May, to 1978

By

Emily T Dugdale

For Sophie and Madeleine - A bond for life.

Author's Note and Trigger Warning

I began writing this book when I was 14 and at the time of publishing, I'm about to turn 20. It has been a labour of love; something creative to keep me going through the hardest challenges of my life. I would write for a while, then get too sick to continue, but the world I created and my beloved characters were always waiting. They're my friends.

The world I've created is set in the very real and very tumultuous midwest of America in the 1950s. I've always been fascinated with the past and whilst it is a love story, I couldn't ignore the issues of my setting. I wanted my book to be representative of a time in which people who were different were often victims of violence and discrimination. The hardships faced by the characters are at the forefront of my narrative, and that is why I wanted to include a trigger warning for anyone who may be affected by this.

The book includes descriptions of violence of a sexual, homophobic and racist nature. There are also mentions of pregnancy loss, abuse, drugs and suicide. Antagonistic characters also use LGBTQIA+ slurs and racial slurs are implied.

Contents

Prologue

In this story, the story of my life, people get hurt, sometimes deeply. When I started to write, I considered leaving parts out. But this is life. My life. As the seasons of our lives change, so do the people we hold dear. Some people live and some people die. Some of us will see more pain than others. I kept writing because life is full of sadness but it is also full of love, and my story is no different.

The seven of us.
Joe, a gentle James Dean with cigarettes in the hollowed-out heels of his fake DocMartins and a box under his bed full of suspension slips. Street-smart but tender. He was all I aspired to be and claimed to have slept with more girls than he had fingers and toes. It was probably true.

Kevin and Donald, the twins- or more commonly known to the inner circle: Kev and Don. They were your usual next-door neighbour types who I had been forced to play with when I was younger, but who became two of my greatest friends. They aren't in my story for long, but I loved them fiercely. They existed in a world built for others and faced hatred that I could never understand.

My best friend in the whole world, Hal. A top-set scholar, destined for some Ivy League School and exactly one month older than me. He thought he knew more of the world than me, and at the time, he did. He kept more secrets than he should have and shared more than was wise.

My brother Finn, three years older than me and built like a tank, was the ringleader (or so he thought), who snuck vodka into the den and stole the ciggies from the hollowed-out heels of Joe's fake DocMartins. It was all part of his image though. He was a jock, the best football player at

Rushford High. Plus, our family was nice and respectable. Boring, but respectable.

Me- Sam, scrawny and small for my age with nothing to brag about except my Dennis the Menace comic strip collection. That was it.

Last but by no means least, was May. She had a wise head on her shoulders and empathy in spades. She also joked her real name was Mayonnaise. May always did the unexpected, with a new hairstyle most days and a completely different wardrobe every time we saw her.
She fussed over us, telling us what to do and how to act, and we loved it. In the end, each of us had our way of loving her.

I remember her perfectly, before what happened... happened. My descriptions of us now were in the summer of 1960, when everything was normal. But that isn't the whole story, of course, so to truly understand what happened later, you must understand what happened first.

Summer Vacation, 1953

Hal and I built a den. It was the best den our eight-year-old brains could dream up. It was made of old wood that Hal and his dad had brought down in his '***Burbank and Sons, Renovators- if we can't do it, no one can***!' truck to the bank of a certain river that I can't for the life of me recall the name of, despite the fact I spent most of my adolescence paddling in it. I must have been told the name in passing when I was a kid and not bothered to listen. I just knew where it was and the quickest way to get there.

The wood for our den had been removed from an old lady's house and, finding she had no use for it, she gave it to Hal's dad as an extra thank you for taking down her porch. Hal's dad (I always referred to him like that because I never knew what to say, as his wife, Mary, called him Dick and his friends called him Rich) helped us nail the planks into some kind of order, eventually creating a grounded tree-house that tilted precariously over the bank. To be honest, I had expected a proper little house, seeing as that's what Hal's dad did for a living, but both Burbank's seemed so pleased with their efforts that I couldn't help but be excited too.

My mother had cut the sleeves off of two of Finn's old sweaters; stuffed and stitched them, and then stapled them onto some apple crates to be used as stools. We also had a horrible Persian rug that mom had tried and failed to sell after we inherited it from our Great Aunt Millie. Hal's dad had also dug a small hole and lined it with tarpaulin as a place to put our torches and snacks. To us, it was a gateway to new adventures. To anyone else, it was a dangerous shack.

I always said the best thing about our den, and keep that opinion today, was that it never got dirty. During our school vacations, we spent every day and almost every night in it, only returning home to get food and water when our supplies were low and this meant that bugs and mud were never allowed in. After the first time Mother Nature rained off our den camp-out, we attached another tarp on the roof to make our haven waterproof.

One day, shortly after the rain escapade, and after the ground had dried, Hal joined me in the den. He found me sitting dejectedly on a stool, my brows furrowed, staring at the floor as if some great evil had befallen me and my kin. To me, it certainly felt that way. Hal looked at my forlorn face.

"Sammy! Sammy, why do you look like that? Why are you so miserable?" He stood cautiously and very straight at the curtained entrance, gently rubbing the frayed fabric between his slim fingers. He was dressed like he always was. He had a pressed white shirt tucked into pressed, beige shorts that finished above his knees. He also wore pristine knee-length socks and a navy, cashmere sweater with a tie that came in a set with a red one. The ties were his pride and joy. It was his signature look, even in the holidays- though in the winter, he wore pressed, beige, long pants instead.

"Mom said we have to let Finley play in our den."

"Why?" Hal asked, sitting down gently next to me. I shrugged my shoulders, though I was going to tell him regardless.

"Because Finley is older than us and he wants a den like this one, but he hasn't got one, so we have to share ours which is not fair because this is our den, yours and mine!" I fell over my words, laying them in a messy heap at Hal's feet and then burst into tears.

"Sammy, don't be upset about it. Finley might make it better for us because he is older." He put his arm around me and smiled his reassuring smile.

"And, the new kids from downtown have to play with us." I wailed. The night before, I had told my parents that one of the old, derelict bungalows was now occupied. I had seen a football and some teddies outside in a cardboard box and thought this new family must have had a kid. My father's words were,

"Better make him feel included, son. I'll get your brother to go and see if he wants to play with you and Hal. Wouldn't that be nice?"

I replied, "No." and was not allowed any dessert.

A fresh wave of tears erupted, and I wiped my snotty nose on the back of my green sweater that had been knitted by Great Aunt Millie.

"It'll be fine. And anyway, we will be the smart ones, you, me and Finley, so we can be in charge."

"You mean *you* will be the smart one. Then Finley, then me." I said, drying my eyes.

"No, because you see, you are smart for working out that I am smarter than you, which means you will be the second smartest in the den at all times. Finley won't have worked that out. He just thinks he's the smartest because he is three years older when it's actually me. Then you." Hal always knew how to cheer me up.

He had brought some iced buns and a bottle of slightly flat lemonade for our consumption as the afternoon progressed. He suggested waiting for the others to arrive before we started, and I begrudgingly agreed even though I hadn't eaten for a whole hour.

I could see my brother's bright ginger hair through the gaps in the slats. "I can smell you, Finley!" I said as he neared the entrance. He shoved his head through the curtain and scowled.

"No, you can't. I had a bath on Monday!"

Hal looked at him with disgust.

"It's Saturday!" Hal said, wrinkling his nose and taking a large step away from him.

"Oh... What I meant to say was... I'll... have a bath on Monday!"

"That's even further away!"

"No one asked you, Hal." Finley pushed his way inside, and despite the fact it was rather a large den, he managed to knock over the lemonade and crash into a stool.

"Of course not. You didn't ask anyone anything. It was a statement." Hal folded his arms and sniffed.

"A what? Oh, I'll thump ya, I swear to God." Finn glared at him.

Before either of them could say anything else, two dark-haired, dark-skinned boys appeared at the entrance to the den shouting my name and brandishing a Cowboys and Indians play set.

I was young and didn't pay attention to discrimination in the news. My parents were always somewhat cold when the twins came to our house to play, but seeing as we spent most of our time in the den, there wasn't much they could do about us being friends. But that day, they were just seven-year-old boys that I didn't know yet. I waved hello and they waved back- that simple gesture giving us a lasting friendship.

They introduced themselves as Kev and Don. Their parents had just moved the family from another town close by. We learned this was because the twins' father was a pastor and he had been called to create a church here. Finn asked who had been on the phone when their father was called but they didn't know. Hal chuckled to himself and glanced at me amused. I smiled back, but I didn't understand Finn's blunder either.

We were all great friends by the evening. We had devoured the iced buns and lemonade for our nutritious evening meal and spent the rest of the day swinging out over the river on a rope swing and trying not to fall into its cold depths. The consensus was that we wanted to stay the night in the den, so after a nerve-wracking game of rock, paper, scissors, to determine who pulled the metaphorical short straw- of course, it was *me* who walked back along the

track to get food for the next day and to inform the adults who were on the need to know basis.
I hummed a tune to myself, Mr Sandman if I remember correctly. My feet hurt in my hand-me-down sneakers and it was too hot for the time of day. But I was happy. How could I not be? I was eight years old.

I could describe in detail how I went home and got the food and told the adults, and I could describe the rest of that summer with the five of us playing in the den. I could describe the day we went back to school, and how heart-breaking it was not to spend our time by the river, pretending to be knights and kings with sticks for swords and lances or cowboys and Indians with sticks for guns and spears. I could even describe the day Kev broke his arm falling from the rope swing and how we lied to his mom and said he fell over on the way home, and nowhere near our precious den. But I won't. Not that it isn't worth describing, it was a great summer, one of the best I've ever had, but... I want to get to the part about May.

In the middle of the school year, 1955

I was ten, and that was much better than being nine, and much, much better than being eight. Finn was thirteen and had been picked for the football team after school on a Tuesday. Mom had asked Finn if he would take me along to one of his practices, and he agreed until she left to get groceries. Then he had just laughed and pushed me down the stairs, declaring I was a "Cock-sucking fag."
The start of the last year and a half hadn't held much excitement for any of us, except for Finn. He had discovered the lock on the bathroom door, and ten-year-old me didn't understand why he took a sock and a magazine in with him and didn't come out 'til teatime.

Kev and Don were struggling in school. They were always together; their bond was unbreakable, but this was perfect ammunition for the kids at school to bully them. I thought this was the only reason they were picked on, not realising that their skin was the main issue in the eyes of my classmates. Iowa didn't have segregated schools, so the twins were forced into a place that was supposed to protect them, but did so on paper only. I told them to try sitting apart at recess but they didn't want to. They only had each other.

Hal had been put in a special 6th-grade math class over the road at the middle school, despite both of us being in 5th grade. He said it was hard and that he wanted to move back down, but I knew he only said it to make me feel better. A few days after Hal switched classes, I came down with Tonsillitis and had to have them removed, and I was off school for four weeks. Hal came to visit me once a week on a Sunday after his mandatory church session. He told me how his math class had taken an interesting turn when a new kid had transferred from a behavioural correction school in Nebraska. He also said that the school hadn't done a very good job in correcting him, as he was always swearing and getting detentions. Apparently, he was one more miss-step away from being suspended already. I couldn't speak, so I wrote down my words on a pad of paper:

"What's his name?"

"Joe Castro."

"Has he moved to town then- if he goes to the school?"

"Yes, right next door to Kevin and Don! They moved from the Bronx."

I shook my head as if to say, "What's that?" and he understood.

"It's in New York."

"I thought you said he was from Nebra..." he put his hand over my pen.

"No, I said his school was in Nebraska. He is originally from New York, and his family is from Guatemala." He saw my blank expression. "This is why you are still doing elementary-level geography! It's in South America. His parents moved to New York, and he was sent to the correction school. Then they had to move, and he was doing fine, so they took him out."

A thought struck me.

"How d'you know that?" I croaked. Hal looked at the floor in silence, chewing his lip. I kicked his arm and he looked up but didn't catch my eye.

"Oh, Miss Brownstein put him next to me," he said flippantly, waving his hand as if it was nothing. "I think it was so I could model behaviour for him. And, well... we got to talking and... he's coming with me to the den this afternoon." I looked at him in complete shock. Tears sprang up and I turned away to hide them. I didn't want Hal to see me upset, in case he thought I was jealous; I was. "Look, he's different from the others...interesting...but I think you will like him! He's clever." I didn't reply, just rolled onto my side and closed my eyes, feigning tiredness as an excuse to get this traitor out of my bedroom.

Two weeks later, I was up and about again, and after a solid hour of begging my mom to let me go, I raced down the track to our den. It was a warm July day, but not as hot as it could have been, and I liked that. The weather couldn't make up its mind whether it wanted to be the middle of summer or the start of an early onset fall. I skipped because no one could see me, but I tried to put some Elvis Presley swagger into my jaunt in case someone could. In hindsight, I would have punched myself really, really, hard in the face, because I looked like an ageing man who had soiled himself.
As soon as I saw the den, I cut the skip and kept the swagger, because even though I wanted to hate this Castro kid, I wanted him to like me.

Joe was tall for an eleven-year-old, and when he grew up, he was tall for a twenty-five-year-old. He towered above me, and I gulped, staring up at him- a scrawny cliché. He had dark oiled hair in a quiff that made him look even older. His skin was caramel and his eyes were dark and deep. To me, he was reminiscent of the guys on the billboards advertising Brylcreem- the guys we all wanted to be.
"I'm Joe. And you must be Sammy." He spoke with a strong New York accent, but there was a hint of something else in the mix. "Nice to meet ya." I shook the hand he offered me and was surprised at how strong his grip was. I almost forgot he was only a year older than me and Hal. And, as much as I wanted to, I couldn't hate him.

I sat in between Kev and Don, so I didn't look too eager to buddy up with Joe. Of course, Finn was talking loudly and making up stories about all the girls he was "gonna do". I could tell that Joe knew it was a load of crap, but he listened with a smirk anyway.
"So," Finn had rolled up his grey shirt sleeves- it was once white- over a pathetic excuse for a bicep and was (not very)

subtly flexing. "Where did you get your jacket? I've got one yanno." Lie.
"My old man gave it to me. Means I'm parta the gang. I mean, Iowa's gotta get its ciggies somehow, am I right?" he laughed when he saw our shocked expressions. "Nah I'm just funnin' ya. I stole it." He laughed again, and the sound was raspy as if those ciggies he had joked about were all too real.
"Nice." Finn puffed out his chest and I rolled my eyes. I looked at Hal. He hadn't spoken much, and I could tell he was regretting introducing Joe to Finn. It secretly made me pleased that Hal was uncomfortable, although I never admitted it.

I tried to remain angry with Hal for introducing a stranger into the gang, but all of us liked him. He was accepting of Kev and Don, Hal was in his good books because he helped him with math, and Finn talked to Joe about girls and cigarettes and other things that they shouldn't have known. He treated me with a respect that I didn't think I truly deserved, as he was this God of girls and booze and I was a tiny mortal that hadn't hit puberty yet.

That evening was much cooler, and a light mist crept over the river, but nothing could dampen our spirits. Joe had a rusty bike that he claimed he had inherited from Al Capone after a hand of poker in The Bronx, even though everyone (just Hal) knew that Capone operated in Chicago, not New York- and we took turns in riding up and down the dirt track whilst blindfolded with Hal's trademark blue tie. Joe jumped on Hal and yanked the tie from around his neck when he had at first refused to give it up peacefully. After, Hal kept on rubbing his neck where Joe had accidentally scratched him in their scuffle. I tried to be sympathetic, but as I said, part of me was ready to be angry about the whole thing.

Don was balanced on the handlebars and Finn was pedalling furiously down the road back to town, with Joe and Kevin whooping and racing behind.

"My mom is going to kill me." I turned around to see Hal standing before me. His arms were slightly out from his sides, showcasing the dust and grass stains now ingrained into his pants and shirt. He looked more dishevelled than I had ever seen him, and I knew it pained him to get dirty.

"Hal, it isn't that bad. Your mom'll just wash them."

"It was washing day on Saturday."

"Oh." That was as far as my sympathy could stretch. "Do you wish you didn't invite Joe then?" I tried my best not to smile and posed it as a serious question.

"No, not inviting him, just Finn... Oh, there's no need to be so smug." I should have known he would notice. "No, it's not that. I just want to be in charge still."

"You are," I said, lightly punching his arm. "You are the smartest boy I know."

"Being smart has nothing to do with it. Joe has amazing stories and... I want everything to be perfect in our den. Bike riding was not on the list for the weekend."

"You worry too much. Come on. You are supposed to tell me what to do, not the other way around!" We walked slowly back into town, talking about the unimportant things that best friends talk about when they are ten.

August, 1955

A few months later, summer vacation rolled around again, and I noticed that Hal was spending less and less time with us, always making up excuses. For Finn's birthday, we went carting, and Hal claimed he had to finish a science project. Finn didn't care at all; he had only invited Hal and the twins because mom said that I had to have someone to talk to whilst Finn zoomed about with his friends from football.

They were all muscular and strong, and I felt very intimidated by them. Only Joe was properly included in their antics. We watched in horror as Joe handed round L&M filters that he pulled out from his hollowed-out heels and lit them up with a swanky Ronson lighter that I knew he couldn't have... or shouldn't have been able to afford. I felt resentment toward the whole group of them. I played it off as disgust for their jeering and profanity but really it was due to the fact that all I wanted was to be included.

I loved the twins, but being a year younger, they weren't as invested in the older boys' activities, instead, they drew pictures in the dust and raced each other up and down the track. I felt a need to be part of Finn and Joe's circle, and as I watched them light up, I marched over, my heart pounding as if it was going to jump out of my chest. I held my skinny hand out and they all glared at me. Charlie smelled strongly of aftershave and even though his left eye twitched continuously, he was still intimidating. Robert was worse. He smelled of sweat and he was even bigger than Finn, who was almost a foot taller than me anyway.

"What the fuck are you doing dweeb? Where's your faggy friend?" Finn leant against the wooden bleachers and flexed his non-existent biceps. I looked at my brother blankly. "Hal! You dweeb." Same insult twice. He was slacking.

I tried to stand up as tall as I could. “Uh, he’s busy.”
“Good. Don’t want that faggot around here anyway.” My brother glared at me, flicking ash onto my shoes. I walked forwards and Charlie stepped in front of me like a wolf blocking a threat from reaching its leader.

“He’s cool.” Joe put a strong hand on Charlie’s arm and I could see a slight annoyance on his face, directed towards Finn. “Want one Sammy?” He held out a cigarette and I hesitated before taking it.
I knew. I did know it was stupid. I put it to my lips and Robert lent down and lit it. I was overwhelmed by the smell of his body odour and my eyes watered even before the taste of smoke hit me. I took a long drag but coughed straight away and all but Joe roared with laughter. I doubled over trying to get fresh air back into my lungs but Joe grabbed me by the arm and dragged me back to Kev and Don. He dumped me in the dirt and shook his head, his oiled hair still perfect.
“What the fuck a’ya playin’ at Sammy? Gonna get ya self killed.”
“One fag won’t kill him, Joe!” Kevin said. He was trying to defend me, but I heard the quiver in his voice.
“Wasn’t on ‘bout the fags.” He looked back toward the posse of turds and sighed. From my position on the ground, I couldn’t see them advancing. “Go home, Sammy...” I didn’t heed his warning and lay in the dust, coughing. There was water in my eyes, but I could see the blurry figures of Kevin and Don getting smaller and smaller.
“What the...” I said, wheezing.

The first kick knocked the only recently regained air out of my lungs and made my head spin as it bounced on the ground. Another kick was aimed at my head, but Charlie had bad aim and it barely touched me. In that short reprieve, I tried to regain my balance and get up, but Finley kicked me in the crotch and I fell again, tears springing to my eyes. Unfortunately, they realised I had wet myself before I did, and another bout of kicking ensued because I was, and I quote, “a pant pissing baby”.

“I tried to tell ya.” I heard Joe’s words as he turned and walked away, hands in his pockets. I thought he might step in and defend me like before, but that was the thing with Joe: he could get under people’s skin with his words and looks, and it usually worked, but when it came to the real stuff, the physical fight, he was completely out of his depth. And he was right, he did try to tell me.

I’ve included this to show how the dynamics of our group were affected by Joe. He was a smart talker, but despite looking the part, never fought. Finn was as thick as two short planks but could land a mean punch when he wanted. The two balanced each other out, which in a way, built up an air of tension as we had two types of fighters in our midst, but it also meant that Joe could talk us into exciting situations and Finn could fight us out if they got too bad.

It was around this time when Robert’s older brother first let him get high on cocaine. Robert then proceeded to show his friends at football how to do the same. Finn abstained for a few weeks but peer pressure and the lure of one day making money from being a hoarder persuaded him. I didn’t know it then, but it was common knowledge between all of the football boys- and Joe, that Finley Harvitz would stash your coke- for a fee.

Christmas Break, 1955

We had snow. Rather a lot.

In the past year, I had only seen Hal about 5 times outside of school. We thought maybe his mom was still angry about Joe losing her son's trademark blue tie. Regardless, I was ready to confront Mary Burbank, and get my best friend back, so one day during Christmas vacation, I marched up to his front door to argue my case.

Hal's house was large and old-fashioned, the oldest new house in the neighbourhood. Built at the turn of the century, it stretched along a broad driveway that was gravelled, with sprouting shrubs in uniformed beds. His father's renovation business wouldn't have been able to afford it, if not for the money that his mom's father had left in his will. Theirs wasn't exactly a marriage of love.

My knuckles rapped on the frosted glass pane in the front door, because I couldn't reach the doorbell. Mary opened the door in a fashionable green and white floral dress, which nipped in at the waist and gave her bosom an almost triangular appearance.

"Samuel! How lovely!"

I peeled my eyes away from her breasts and said hurriedly, "G'morning Mrs Burbank, now, I know Hal is supposed to be..." but she cut me off.

"Looking for our Henry? Let me get him, honey! You'll need some help shovelling snow out of that den of yours!" She hopped with a springing step away from the open door and called up the staircase. "Henry! Samuel is here!" I stood there stunned, not knowing quite what to make of it. Either Mrs Burbank had changed her tune, or the tune had never altered in the first place.

I heard Hal's voice drift down from above.

“Tell them I’m busy mom. I’ll hang out with the others next weekend or something. Tell them to leave. Please.”

“No, no it’s just Samuel here, I can’t ask him to go on his own.”

“Oh.” I heard movement, and soon Hal and I were walking in silence away from his house. Me in just my jacket and him bundled up and laden to the high heavens in scarves and various other knitted articles of clothing.

“So... your mom said you weren’t feeling so well last weekend.” I broached the subject carefully.

“Hm? Sorry, I wasn’t listening.”

“The reason you didn’t come to Kev and Don’s party? Your mom said you were sick.” He looked flustered and he swallowed a few times before speaking.

“Oh yes, I had a headache I think.” We walked a bit longer before I called him out.

“Hal, what the fuck is going on?” My language surprised us both, as I had never sworn in front of him before. “Your mom didn’t say you were sick, she said you had a geography project last week. Why did you lie? Why won’t you hang out with us?”

He looked shocked that I had spoken so openly. He seemed about to speak, then closed his mouth and walked a few paces before stopping and turning around.

“Do you ever think about girls Sammy?” The abruptness of the question took me by surprise.

“Uh, I guess? They’re nice to look at and all but...” I trailed off, not sure what he wanted me to say.

“I don’t.”

“Don’t what?”

"Think they're nice to look at."

"Oh. Maybe you just haven't seen enough girls yet."

"Maybe. Do you think about them in...other ways? How Finley and Joe do?"

"Nah. I mean... I don't think so. They're pretty or whatever. But I wouldn't kiss one or anything."

"I see." He turned and carried on walking. I had to accept that I wasn't going to get a straight answer from him. He was cryptic, and I was not.

I never apologised for my outburst, but our friendship became stronger after that day shovelling snow. Hal hung out with us a lot more, though a part of me suspected it was out of duty to start with- so he wouldn't look like he was avoiding us.

August, 1959

I was 14. My voice cracked occasionally which got me a lot of abuse from Finn and Joe. Certain parts of me grew, and others- unfortunately- didn't. I naively felt older than I was, but I looked a lot younger.

Hal was starting to look like a man. He wasn't as broad or muscular as Joe and Finn, but he was now even taller than me and his voice had already dropped. Kev and Don were still kids, but they had a certain intelligence from having to grow up fast in a world that hated them.

Finn's friends got high a lot that summer, with Finn stashing the drugs in his sock drawer for when someone hit him up with business. Finn claimed he did coke with Joe, Robert, Charlie, and the other footballers, but he didn't do it regularly- not yet. He needed his spot on the team more than they did and if he was caught on strong stuff, his future was in jeopardy before he even graduated.

We still hung out in the den, though now we read porn and smoked instead of beating each other up with sticks and paddling in the river. I had gotten better at holding my smoke, and now I hardly coughed at all. Hal never touched it.

Joe once brought four packs in his shoes and handed them around. Hal shook his head and went back to reading Lord of the Flies.

"Pussy." Said Joe. He laughed, and Finn joined in, hitting Hal hard on the shoulder. It was meant as a joke- from Joe, not Finn- but I could see that it hurt him. He shrugged it off but after the conversation had returned to the breasts in Joe's magazine, Hal stood up quietly and walked outside. I was the only one who seemed to notice, so reluctantly left the picture of a model who looked eerily like Hal's mom, and followed him.

He was sitting on a log about 10 yards away from the den. I could hear whooping and dirty jokes behind me, but my best friend needed me more than they did.

His hair was combed perfectly as ever, and he wore his trademark outfit, but this time, a deep red and brown version of the same. He was impeccable but there was a sadness in him today.

"Do you know what happens in Lord of the Flies, Sammy?" He didn't turn to look at me; he seemed to know I was there.

"No. Yanno I haven't read that shit."

He didn't even defend his book, just jumped straight in with his cryptic clues that I didn't understand.

"These boys end up stranded. They try to form some sort of society, but obviously, it fails, and they rip each other to shreds. Literally. That's what is happening here, Sammy. Them, in there," he waved a hand vaguely towards the den, "are growing up, but they aren't grownups. They have no idea what it's actually like. In the real world." I stood silently, watching his side profile and his Adam's-apple bobbing as he spoke. "Eventually, we will tear ourselves apart. We can't sustain this kind of friendship. They can't ..." his voice cracked with emotion and I reached out and put my hand on his shaking shoulder. "Do you understand?" He said, gazing at me desperately.

"No. You're talkin' bullshit again." I shuffled my feet. Hal sniffed, amused. "You should come back in Hal; the others will wonder where we got to," I said. He didn't move. I laughed awkwardly and lightly pushed him. "Come on, don't be a fag."

He shrugged my hand away and stood abruptly. "Is that what you think?" His voice was angry but his eyes were exhausted.

"What? No, I was just..." My newly loosed hormones readied me for a fight, but Hal looked so defeated.

"Yeah, I know." He sighed and stared at the den for a long moment. "I should go. Pot roast for supper."

"You can't leave now! We were gonna stay the night!"

He looked undecidedly at the den again and then back at me. Suddenly a look of confusion flashed across his normally unflustered features. "What was that?"

I went to speak but he put a finger to his lips.

Twigs snapped nearby, and the unmistakable rustle of leaves pricked my ears.

"It'll be a fox, Hal," I said, though a part of me feared a wolf or something else we definitely couldn't fight- not that I think we could have fought a fox. We both edged our way forward, inching towards a large oak where the noise was emanating from. Just as we were about to pounce and scare off the creature, the creature strolled around the tree and scared us.

A girl. Fair-skinned and bright, with dark hair that caught the light, causing brown and auburn highlights to flash along the strands as she looked us up and down. It was secured with brass pins in a loose bun. Tendrils and curls escaped and fell, framing her chiselled face. She was so close I could see into the depths of her eyes- light grey pools of mist that gazed and saw everything that you didn't want her to know. Her lips were naturally a rosy pink and when she smiled at the two of us, my heart melted for the first time.

She wore high-waisted, navy pants that finished above her ankles and on her feet, she wore tan and white Oxfords and white socks that were embroidered with little bows. A loose-fitting, flouncy, white shirt was tucked into the pants and a red scarf was tied fashionably around her neck. She was a movie star. She was beautiful.

Other than in movies and magazines, I had never seen anyone like her. The glossy pages and silver screens seemed so distant and untouchable, that I had convinced myself that such beauty was confined to mysterious women in far-off places.

"Oh!" she stepped back in alarm, but instantly her face melted into a warm, beautiful smile, as she realised we were (definitely) not a threat. Hal and I were still a little shocked, but Hal recovered quickly and returned the smile. I, foolishly, tried to lean against a nearby tree to look cool but my foot slipped, and my leg went down a fox hole.

I cried out and the girl lunged forward and grabbed me just in time to stop my entire torso from being enveloped by the earth.

"Careful sweetie." Her voice was clear and deep. She picked me up, and Hal helped her walk me back to the den.

"Um, thanks," I said, blushing.

"No problem- just make sure you look where you're putting your feet next time! The name's May." She looked at us both with her teasing smirk that I would become so used to in the future. Hal held out his perfectly clean hand.

"My name is Henry, but everyone calls me Hal. It's a pleasure, miss."

She laughed a brilliant, beautiful laugh. She looked at her feet, her head tilted to the side, and then her gaze returned to Hal.

"The pleasure is all mine sweetie. Hasn't my little walk turned out well!" She pivoted and was suddenly very close to me. "And you are?"

My mouth was dry, and I couldn't get the words out. I just stared at her, my heart pounding out of my chest.

"Um, is he okay?" She winked at Hal and flicked her hair effortlessly off her face. She was joking, but I was embarrassed. I nodded my head hurriedly and pulled myself together.

"Sammy. Sam. I'm Sam." I thrust out my hand to shake hers but she was so close that I ended up jabbing her in the chest.

"Woah, second base and we've only known each other for 5 minutes!" She laughed again and brushed past me, putting her hand on the wall of the den. I stood dumbfounded, not quite sure which way was up. "What's this neat lil' construction?" I loved her even more for not calling it a shack.

Hal stepped forward, taking charge of the situation. "It's our den. The six of us spend almost every day here."

"I see. It's lovely," she stroked the wall as if she had been its architect. "The six of us?" She asked.

As if on cue, Finn, Joe and the twins fell out of the door in a heap. I would have laughed if I hadn't been almost comatose.

Joe dusted himself off, still managing to look effortless whilst fishing a leaf out of his oiled hair. Finn was flailing his arms around sporadically, swearing and shouting at the twins. He jumped to his feet and shoved Don into the dirt.

"You put ya foot in my mouth you asshole. Fuck you." Kev bravely stepped in front of his brother and pulled him up. Finn raised his fist, ready to land a hard blow on Kevin's chin, but stopped dead when he saw May. He made a kind of grunting noise and automatically puffed out his chest. Noticing that Hal and I were closer in proximity to her, he took three large strides, pushed us both aside and breathed his gross breath right in her face. "Hiya gorgeous." He was dressed like Joe, white t-shirt tucked into circulation-cutting jeans and black DocMartins, except he looked like a wannabe. Joe pulled off the James Dean wardrobe with ease.

Introductions were made, and Finn made some rude gestures to Joe about what he wanted to do to May behind her back- quite literally. It wasn't very subtle, but if she noticed, she never said.

We sat in the den, the porn shoved under a rug, and talked for hours. Us boys sat in a semicircle, facing her like disciples. She spoke, and we focused on every single thing: the way she said certain words, how her mouth moved, the way she adjusted her legs when she had been sitting too long- all of it.

"I moved from my half-sister's place in Des Moines about three weeks ago. My aunt is renting an apartment on the Hallingham estate near Rushford High. I'm staying with her and her guy Derek until I finish school. I'm going into fashion." She looked at us expectantly and we all 'oo-ed' and 'ah-ed'.

Kevin piped up, "what about your parents?" and she was silent for a few seconds.

"My mom... died last fall. And I never had a dad. Mom met him on holiday in Florida and came back with more than a postcard."

"Oh, I'm sorry..." Kevin tried to apologise but she waved her hand dismissively.

"S'kay sweetie. You couldn't have known. I'm better off without my dad. Knocked up my mom and then refused to marry her. He sends me a check twice a year, at birthdays and Christmas, and that's all the contact I need!" she stretched and sighed. "Anyone got a ciggie?"

Joe and Finn scrambled under the stools for a pack, pinching each other to come out on top. Joe prevailed and offered the pack to May, and she leaned over me, her hand accidentally brushing my face. I breathed her in as she selected her cigarette and stretched out on the rug, lying on her back, one leg raised. She fished a lighter out of her pocket. “I like you guys, but I’ll take my smoke and go. I don’t wanna intrude on your den and all your... boy stuff.”

“Stay!” we all said in unison, causing her to smirk.

“Well only if you’re sure, sweeties.” She reached inside her shirt and pulled a miniature bottle of whiskey from her bra. Unscrewing the top, she beamed at us. “Anyone want a swig?”

All of us but May stayed the night. She left around eight. We didn’t talk about her after she went; all lost in our thoughts. In the early hours of the morning when everyone else was asleep, I felt Finn’s hot breath in my ear. “She’s mine.” I was pretending to be asleep, but a red-hot rage balled inside me and I curled my fist in my sleeping bag. I had been on fire since she stopped me from falling, and his self-confident words fuelled me differently, but with the same effect. “Try anything, and you die.” He growled.

I rolled over suddenly and spat in his face. He was so shocked, that by the time he realised what had happened, I had returned to my previous position on the floor. I waited for the pain of his fist exploding against the back of my head, but the pain never came. Not to me.

At the time, I didn’t think I would see her again, though I hoped I would. She was perfect in my eyes and I couldn’t understand why she would want to spend time with me.

That didn’t stop me from thinking about her every day. She was my first thought in the morning and my last thought at night. She often crept into my thoughts throughout the day too.

I saw her around town from time to time. She did some afternoons in the corner store, and I always took my allowance down in the hopes of bumping into her. She smirked at me when she saw me in the queue, and once she asked me, “What’s goin’ on sweetie?”

I would have bragged about it if I had had anyone to brag to apart from Hal. I saw her at school occasionally but she mostly stayed in the art rooms. She was 15 already, but still in my grade, meaning she was around in assemblies and at recess, but I didn’t see her much.

She was beautiful and seemed elevated above us all, and I didn’t think for a moment that she would come back to the den. But she did.

In late September, I strolled down to the den to meet the twins and Joe. Hal said he had another big project, and Finn had football practice.
I heard them laughing before I saw them. One laugh penetrated my ears, making me smile involuntarily. It was her.
“You won’t do it! She won’t do it!” I heard Kev’s voice shrieking with glee.
“No, no! Don’t, it’s wriggling!” Don screeched. I pulled back the curtain with bemused haste, to see May holding a fat, squirming worm to her lips. The twins were pinned against the far wall, begging her not to do it and giggling incessantly. Joe was lying close to May, showing his amusement in his cool, calm way.
“She’s gonna do it!” Kevin said, covering his eyes. May lowered the worm into her mouth and chewed slowly and triumphantly. An explosion of “Ew! Gross!” was heard from the twins. She swallowed her disgusting mouthful and opened her mouth to prove she had done it. Joe clapped and put his hand on her leg.
“That was nasty, but damn, I do like a girl who can hold stuff in her mouth.” He winked at her.
She brushed his hand away and snorted, “I’d put fifty earthworms in my mouth before I’d let you come near me with yours!”

I had been standing stunned at the entrance this whole time, watching the scene unfold. The sound of my name being called startled me.
“Sammy? Is that you? There’s a glare behind ya. Can’t see.” She beckoned me over and patted the ground next to her.
“May... Hello.” I sat down, feeling self-conscious about my messy hair and faded pants. She noticed me awkwardly running my hands through my matted hair and put a hand on my arm.
“You look positively ravishing sweetie. Don’t fuss.” She said in a fake British accent.
I smiled at her, trying and failing to exude confidence. Joe suppressed a laugh and sidled closer to May.
She was wearing a white and pink checked sun-dress with buttons down the front. Her feet were bare, and her toenails were painted red. I could see her white sandals in the corner.

We talked about this and that. To an outside observer, the conversation would have seemed menial and dull, as May had a habit of talking about herself, but we all hung on her every word. It seems pointless to tell you everything that passed between us, because, in the funny ways of young love, our conversations were indeed menial and dull- I just yearned to hear them anyway.

December, 1959

Every Christmas the Burbank's threw a holiday party for the parents in town, which meant that we kids had a whole evening without adult supervision. It was bitterly cold, but the seven of us wrapped up warm and took extra blankets down to the den. May brought some hot chocolate and Joe had pinched some fancy ginger biscuits from somewhere. It was a nice evening; the snow had stopped and everyone was cosy, but there was a strange atmosphere in the air. Joe was just a little bit too close to May for my comfort. Finn was wide-eyed and jealous of Joe, despite the cash he'd been earning from storing the football team's coke. Kevin and Don were quiet. Kev had a bruise on his cheek and Don had cuts all over his arms, courtesy of Billy Draper from the football team. Hal was unusually sprightly and kept the conversation going. May was happy to indulge him. It upset me that she didn't ask Joe to take his hand off of her thigh.

It's strange how the mind chooses to remember certain things. I remember some days as clearly as I can see the typewriter in front of me, and some... have just faded. I do remember June 1961.

She broke my heart.

June, 1961

I was so happy when my 16th birthday rolled around. I rushed down to the den after family dinner to meet my friends, leaving Finn to make his way alone.

"Sam!" May came out of the den to meet me. She gave me a huge hug and kissed my cheek. I nearly fell over.

She took my hand and led me inside, and I realised no one else was there yet. Hal was going to meet us after his supper. I don't know if it was the adrenaline from her kiss or the fact that my balls had dropped by then, but I decided that this was my chance to tell her how I felt. I opened my mouth to speak, but she thrust a package into my lap before I could utter a single syllable. "I got you a present. Hope you don't mind sweetie."

"Mind? Of course not." I pulled off the baby-blue tissue paper. I held the gift in disbelief.

"S'a camera. Nothing fancy." She looked at me expectantly.

"May... you really shouldn't have."

"Well really, I didn't. Just one that the art department at school didn't need anymore. I thought it'd be nice to get some snaps of us all this summer."

I leaned over and hugged her tightly. "Thank you."

She hugged me back and I breathed in the smell of her hair.

"So, what'd your folks get ya?" She leaned back and smiled.

"Some books."

"Of the comic variety?" She smirked and I blushed. "Sweetie, I'm just playin'. I'm sure they'd rather you read Archie and Veronica than a porno."

"Speaking of..." A voice startled us both. Joe stood in the doorway, with Finn just behind. Joe threw a paper bag at me. I peered inside and spied a familiar-looking magazine. The cover of Playboy for June 1961 was a green motor car with a brunette in the driver's seat- presumably naked. It's strange what you remember.

"What'd ya get?" May asked expectantly. I cleared my throat awkwardly and looked at Joe for help.
"Oh... you know... just some car magazines..." I tried to put the bag behind me, but she lunged for it and pulled it out of my hands. The three of us held our breaths as May pulled out the porn.
"Well, there is a car on the front," she said, half suppressing a smile. "And look here!" she flicked to a random page. "This fine specimen is lounging on a Chevy. Looks as though she's missed a few buttons on her blouse!" Smirking, she handed me back the magazine.
"It's... um... um... it's a car enthusiast special," I said, turning crimson.
"She's hot! I get it." She said leaning back with a smile.
I shoved the magazine under one of the milk crates and hurriedly tried to change the subject.
"Where are the twins?" I asked Finn.
"How the fuck should I know?" He scoffed and then said the one word he should never have said. We all stared at him in shock. None of us had ever called the twins that before. May turned on him.
"What the fuck Finn?"
He puffed out his chest and looked as though he was going to go off at her. Joe put a hand firmly on Finn's arm.
"Cool it, man. Let it go."
Finn shrugged Joe off and sat down heavily. "Give me the fuckin Playboy dickweed." He growled. I threw it at him-anything to shut him up. Mom had told me to go easy on him because the football scholarship he so desperately needed after his graduation the following month was going to his friend Charlie instead.

The rest of us sat in uncomfortable silence. After a few minutes, Joe got up. "I need a piss." May watched him leave and then smiled at me.
"How're you enjoying your birthday Sam?"
I stole a glance at Finn in the corner and she seemed to understand. I'd been angry with Finn all day. He hadn't

said happy birthday to me that morning and when I'd gone looking for my best red socks in his drawer and found the cocaine, he'd grabbed me by the collar and threatened to cut one of my fingers off if I told.
"Hey!" Came Joe's voice from outside, "Someone gimme a fuckin torch. Can't see shit."
"I'll get it!" May shouted back. She picked up the torch and rushed outside, leaving me alone with my brother.

Silence.

"Stop fucking pining after her." He didn't look up from the tits on page 12.
"I'm not," I said defensively.
"Bullshit. We all know you think about her in the shower." He jeered at me, cupping imaginary breasts.
"I do not. You're just jealous that she won't go anywhere near you." I seemed to have hit a sore spot. He jumped up furiously.
"You don't know anything, do you? Fuckin' numbskull." He leaned in close to my face and sneered. "Her and Joe. They're doin' it."
I stared at him in disbelief.
"You're lying."
"Go outside then. Bet she's helpin' him take that piss. Dirty bitch." He went casually back to page 12.
"You're a fucking liar!" I leapt up and marched out of the den to prove to Finn that he was wrong.

Joe was right, you couldn't see anything. I peered into the gloom and saw the flickering torchlight in the distance. I crept carefully towards it, trying not to fall. The light was coming from behind a large oak tree. How far had they gone? I stopped dead. I could hear soft noises in front of me. I walked around the side of the tree and stopped again. May had her back against the trunk, her face contorted in what looked like a scream. I rushed forward to help her, but she cried out.

"Sam! What the fuck?" She sounded angry. It was then that Joe emerged from between her legs.
"You heard the lady. What the fuck Sam?" Joe stood and rolled his shoulders, towering above me. I couldn't form any words. My mouth was completely glued shut. Before I knew what I was doing, I turned and ran back towards the den, tripping clumsily over every root and stone. My heart was pounding and my head was hot. Finn was right. They were doing it. May and Joe. May and Joe fucking Castro. May fucking Joe Castro. I could hear footsteps behind me, but I didn't stop. I reached the den and smashed my fist hard against the wall. Inside, Finn exclaimed loudly and stormed out. I had just about recovered when Joe and May arrived behind me. May opened her mouth to say something but she was cut off by a voice coming from the other direction.

Hal was racing down the track towards us. He stopped and caught his breath. There was a ruggedness to his appearance that wasn't like him at all. His pants were mud-splattered, and his hair was unkempt from running.

"Something has happened."

July, 1961

Kevin James Salim Washington was buried at 4 o'clock on a Wednesday after a service given by his father. His gravestone said that he would be dearly missed. He was.

A few days before my birthday, the twins had been playing in the street outside the corner store, when Kev had accidentally bumped into Mary-Ellen Draper, causing her to drop the milk she was holding. Mary-Ellen went home that night and told her brother Billy. Robert, Charlie, Billy and several other members of the football team had stopped the twins on the way to the den on the evening of my birthday. They pushed the twins to the ground and beat them for twenty minutes. Billy pulled out a knife that he'd stolen from his dad. Don managed to crawl away as the boys pissed on his brother's dead body.

We weren't allowed to go to the funeral, but we saw the tiny coffin go in. We waited outside the twins' church for the service to be over. Joe comforted May on a small bench. We watched Don and his parents get into their car and drive away. They changed their names and moved to Tulsa. I never saw him again.

The cops got involved but the football team wasn't punished. They were let off with a warning. Billy Draper's father was on the force.
Finn didn't go to the church with us. I knew why. The cops had said that the boys on the football team were suspected of being high on cocaine at the time of the attack. And I knew where they'd gotten it from.

September, 1961

Kevin's death and Don's sudden departure to Oklahoma took its toll on our gang, but we all had our ways of dealing with it. Finn could hide his guilt by drinking and getting high with the football team. He abandoned his jock image and started snorting the coke in his sock drawer as well as selling it. He didn't hang out with us anymore.

Hal started spending less and less time with us again. He had made a new friend in his economics class, Desmond Hargreaves.
Joe started seeing a girl from the next town. She let him take nude pictures of her after they'd had sex. He showed them to us and they turned me on.
I cried myself to sleep most nights thinking about Kevin in the Earth and Don in Tulsa and Joe between May's legs.
She pretended as though nothing had changed.

Some of the stories I have written here were told to me after the event. A lot of my memories of Hal's personal life throughout the early sixties are ones created by other people's retellings. As I said, he wasn't around much anymore. I went over to his house to get help with math homework, but the conversation was awkward and forced. The only other times I saw him was with everyone else at the den. It could never just be the two of us. My best friend and me.

At the start of the school year, Hal got a girlfriend. Her name was Nancy Waters. She was a top scholar, like Hal, and did figure-skating in her spare time. Her father was our pastor, meaning she was a very devout Christian and head of the school's chastity club, attending church every Sunday with Hal in tow. That's where they'd met. Over wafers and weak Ribena.

Whenever he came down to the den, Nancy came too. She was pleasant with May, as they both loved clothes, but it was obvious that her openness made Nancy uncomfortable. May didn't seem bothered. I didn't mind her either. It wasn't like she was stealing my friend away. He was doing that all by himself. Plus, Hal didn't interact with Nancy. When they talked it was only pleasantries and I never saw him do as much as hold her hand.

One evening towards the end of September, there was a knock at my door. My mother answered it. I could hear muffled voices from downstairs.
"Joseph! How are you dear? I'll call Finley for you..."
"Evenin' ma'am. Nah, Mrs Harvitz. Sam, actually."
"Oh!" My mother climbed the stairs and opened my bedroom door. "Joseph's here dear. Don't stay out too late, the Burbank's are coming round for pot roast remember!"
I sighed and got up to leave. "Is Hal coming?"
"I believe so. Don't look so moody Samuel. At least try for a smile!"

Neither of us said anything until we had walked past all of the houses on my street and we were on our way to the den. It was unusual for Joe to call on me. We hadn't talked alone since I caught him and May.
"I didn't know we were meeting up today." I ventured, trying to start a conversation.
"We ain't." My silence must have shown my confusion because he sighed and went on. "Look..." He stopped and sat down at the side of the path. He was uncharacteristically subdued. "I got somethin' to tell ya, okay?"
I stood awkwardly in front of him, my hands in my pockets.
"Okay."
"It's Hal."

An image of Kevin's small casket flashed through my mind.
"What? Is he okay?" I said, panicking.

"Shut up an' listen. Si'down." He said. So, I did.
"The other day I was with ya brother and that lot from football. Smokin' on the bleachers like usual, yanno." He paused and ran a hand nervously through his hair. Joe was never nervous. "So Bobby hands me a fag an' the meathead drops the bastard an' it falls under the bleachers. They're expensive, yanno- fags- and Bobby's a big fucker so I say I'll go get it."
He was rambling. I wanted him to hurry up and get to the point, but I could tell he was finding it hard to get the words out.
"I jump down an' crawl on my hands and knees where I reckon the fag shoulda been. I can hear talkin' but I'm thinkin' 's probably the guys above yanno. But I'm gettin' further away from 'em an' I can still hear talkin' an' there's movement in front of me. Hal's there. With that kid that sits behind him in Econ... Edmund?"
"Desmond." I stared at Joe blankly. "And?"
It was Joe's turn to look confused. "Can't ya see where I'm goin' with this Sam?"
"So what? He was with Desmond Hargreaves. Where was he supposed to be?"
"Sam...he was *with* him. Like I'm *with* Linda Grogan when her folks go away or Felicity Fisherwitz under the table in homeroom. Like ya *with* ya hand or a tube sock every night. Ya, see what I'm sayin' Sam?"
I stared at him, not quite sure how to react. "Hal and... they were... doing... *it*?"
Joe shuffled his feet. "Nah... kinda. Hal was on 'is knees an' Arnold,"
"Desmond."
"Yeah... tha's what I said. Desmond. He was leanin' against the side of the bleachers. He had his... thing..."
"Yeah, I get it, Joe." I put my head between my knees and breathed deeply. Why hadn't Hal told me he was... "I don't believe you. This some prank you and Finn thought up? Huh?" I stood and kicked a large stone across the path. "You gotta be making this up."

"I ain't Sam. Hal heard somethin' and saw me a few yards away. He ran after me pretty fast but I'm faster." He shook his head. "I ain't lyin'. Why d'ya think he's datin' the head of the chastity club? Huh? So 'e don't havta touch her Sam."
It all made sense. I felt sick. "Have you told anyone?"
"Nah. Just you. Thought you oughta be the one to sort 'im out. Tell 'im he can't be treatin' a nice girl like Nancy this way yanno. Tell 'im it ain't natural Sam."
"Okay." We sat in silence for what felt like an eternity but couldn't have been more than a few minutes. "I don't think I can say anything to him." I wrung my hands nervously.
"Huh? Why?"
"What am I supposed to say, Joe? He's a fucking..." Joe interrupted me.
"I know. But... it's Hal. Gotta sort 'im out before Nancy hears a rumour or somethin'. Dunno what that Bernard..."
"Desmond."
"...Desmond will say, yanno."

That evening, the Burbank's came over for a pot roast. Mrs Burbank brought a flan that looked like the inside of a zit. Mr Burbank brought some ale he'd brewed- it was his latest venture. Hal brought some chemistry homework.
After some polite dinner conversation, my father excused us boys from the table and we went silently upstairs. Hal sat at my desk and worked through his complicated questions on alkanes and alkenes and I lay angrily on my bed, throwing a small ball at the ceiling. Hal flinched every time the ball made contact, but I didn't stop. We hadn't said more than a few pleasantries all evening; I kept replaying Joe's words in my head.

I'd thought about sex before. I'd seen models in pornos, and they danced around my dreams frequently. Sometimes May popped into my head. I didn't like thinking about her in that way. It's not that I didn't want to unzip her yellow sundress and see everything, it was just that it felt wrong. She wasn't as untouchable as the women in magazines. She was real. I felt like she'd know if I explored myself while pretending it was her on me. She'd see into my mind. But I'd never thought about it being between guys. I couldn't picture it. It didn't make sense. I was angry. But now the image of Hal *with* Desmond was carved into my mind like knife marks in butter. I lay there, feeling my blood boil until I couldn't hold it in any longer.

"Hal."

He jumped. "Yes?" He didn't look up, his pencil merely falling still.

"How's Nancy?"

"Fine." He stiffened slightly but carried on working. I let a few moments of silence hang in the empty air.

"Anything new?"

He flipped the pencil he was using to erase a line of numbers. "Nothing of note. Her friend Lynn keeps asking about you though. Maybe she likes you."

"Uh-huh." I could picture Nancy's friend. Sweet, but plain. I threw the ball at the ceiling a few more times. Hal shuffled in his chair.

"Why do you ask?"

"Oh...yanno. Just wondering. Thought she might have heard some *stuff* going around."

"What stuff?"

"Dunno." I got up and walked over to my desk. I picked up an 'Archie and Veronica' and casually went back to my position on the bed. "I saw Joe today."

Hal lay his pencil carefully on the paper. "Oh?" His voice was shaky. "What did he have to say then?"

"Not a lot. Just wanted a talk about a few things."

"Oh?"

"He seemed to think that you and that Hargreaves kid have been getting kinda... close."

"Yes, well we both like econ and science so we help each other out at the weekends..." still speaking, he turned to look at me, but he saw the anger on my face. "Sam, I don't want to play games. Please... just say what you're going to say." He sounded small and defeated. He knew.

"How could you?" I couldn't meet his gaze.
"I don't know!" he implored. "It was a mistake. A one-time thing, I swear."
"Why'd you do it? What about Nancy, what if she found out... what you are?"
"You haven't told..."
"No."
He breathed a sigh of relief. "Thank you."
I ignored him. "You care about Nancy then?" He nodded furiously. "And you only did it once." Nod. "Why?"
"Well..." he fiddled with his shirt cuffs nervously, seemingly trying to come up with an excuse. "Her father is a minister. And..." He glanced at the floor and tapped his feet with apprehension. He didn't appear to believe his own story. "She is very, *very* religious. She wasn't going to..."
"...Fuck you?" He nodded again. "But why a guy, Hal? You'll go to hell!"
"Don't say that. Don't!" He whispered furiously. With surprising speed, he rushed towards me and grabbed me by the collar. His face was red; he was angrier than I had ever seen him. I thought he might hit me, but he remembered himself and let go. "I think Nancy is swell. I think lots of girls are swell." He was quieter now. "But I don't love her. I don't want to... with her."
"You love... Desmond Hargreaves?"
"No! It was just... I *swear* it won't happen again. Look, I... I just want to get better." He began to cry quietly.
I softened and put my arm around him. "I want to help you. Try with Nancy. And if she won't give it up... there are plenty of others. That oughta sort ya right out."

I hate writing it.

But that is what happened. In 1961 I was just a boy who was trying to save his friend from the damnation he was told awaited people like him. Now, I'm an old man who just wants his best friend back.

Hal kept seeing Nancy as I suggested, and he seemed happy. I kept my promise and didn't tell anyone, but the truth always comes out.

November, 1961

On the second Tuesday of every month, the town hall held a bingo night. My parents attended every event, without fail. Finn and I elected to stay at home. Me, so I could read my comic books, and Finn, so he could easily sneak out to smoke and get high with his friends.

On that particular Tuesday, I came home from the comic book store to find May on the porch. She sat on the top step, huddled in a brown camel coat and rolling snowballs with her heavy boots. As soon as she saw me her face lit up.

"My knight in shining armour!" She pretended to faint. "I am so very cold, please rescue me!"

I smiled and unlocked the door as she hugged me hard from behind. The house was dark, meaning Finn wasn't home.

"Cocoa?" I asked as she took off her coat. She was wearing deep red slacks and a white blouse that framed her figure perfectly. She caught me staring.

"Only if you make 'em slutty." She smiled and winked at my father's liquor cabinet. I went into the kitchen and made the drinks, but when I came back, she wasn't there. I could hear music coming from upstairs. She was in my room and had turned on the radio. A piano played alongside a saxophone. It sounded so tinny and far away.

"Thank you, sweetie," she said, taking a sip. "I hope you don't mind me coming up. Just wanted to see where the wild Sam lurks." She lay back on my bed. "It's nice."

"Why are you here, May?" I didn't mean to sound sharp, but I was nervous. I always was around her.

"Your brother is supposed to be here. We're going to the pictures."

"Oh." My face felt hot and tears stung involuntarily behind my eyes. I'd assumed she was here to see me. "Well... he's not. Our folks are at bingo, so he's out... doing stuff."

"Getting high, no doubt. Shoulda known. Ah well. We can have some fun though, can't we Sam?"

"Uh, yeah." I perched on the bed next to her and she stretched her legs across my lap. Her shirt had come untucked in one place and I could see some of her stomach. I swallowed nervously, "What d'ya wanna do then?"
She pouted and looked around my childish bedroom, searching for something, anything, that would be to her taste.
"Dance. I wanna dance." She swung her legs off the bed, got up, and turned the dial on the radio. Slow, moany piano echoed around my bedroom. She started swaying to the music.
"I dunno how to dance," I said, holding my hands up in protest.
"Sure ya do! Finn's told me all about how when you were young your ma taught ya how to dance for when you're gettin' hitched."
She was right. "Fine."
She exclaimed in delight and clapped her hands. Doris Day started to sing as I stood up and tentatively put my hands on May's waist. I felt awkward and she knew it.
"Just relax honey." She put her arms around my neck and moved gracefully to the beat, pushing her hips against me. My cheeks flushed and the room's temperature seemed to increase rapidly. "Hello, you." She smirked.
"Uh, hi?" I said, confused.
"Wasn't talking to you..." she glanced down.
"Shit!" I jumped back. "I'm sorry... fuck... fuck... sorry..." I felt like bursting into tears. I backed away from her and sat sheepishly down on my bed.
"Honey... it's okay." She sat slowly down next to me. I couldn't look at her. "No need to apologise." She rested her hand on my belt buckle.
My heart was beating out of my chest; I felt faint. She walked her fingers along my belt, edging closer to my zipper. A tingle shuddered up my spine and I whimpered involuntarily. She laughed and put her other hand on my cheek, bringing my face close to hers.

Then she kissed me.

My whole body was engulfed in fire. I was frozen but burning up.
A door slammed. May broke away from our embrace and inhaled sharply.
"Shit! Finn!" She wiped her mouth and straightened her blouse. I stared at her numbly. "I gotta go Sam." With that, she leapt up and ran out of my room. I didn't stop her. I couldn't breathe, let alone speak.
Finn was in his bedroom. I could hear him rummaging around in his sock drawer for more coke. May's voice was raised above the racket.
"Hey, honey. I've been waiting."
I lay back on my bed, breathing heavily. I replayed what had just happened and tried to calm my heartbeat. I could hear May and my brother talking softly in the next room. The odd word carried through the wall. May was asking where he'd been and he wouldn't say. I stayed completely still on my bed for what seemed like an age but couldn't have been more than 2 minutes. My left hand pondered the open zipper, gently tracing the outline of my still erect penis. I pulled my hand away and clenched my fist. No. It felt wrong. Didn't it?

The voices from Finn's room had fallen silent. I wondered if May had left. But then, I heard a dull thud, followed by a second bang a beat later. The noise continued and I realised what it was. Finn's headboard. I sprung to my feet and pushed myself against the furthest wall away from the noise. I felt like screaming. How could she kiss me and then... they know I'm in the house. Is this some kind of torture?
My only thought was getting out of the house. It was dark, and there was ice on the roads, but I didn't care. I pulled on a pair of boots and a jacket and ran out into the night. I slipped on the top porch step and fell down the rest, bruising my coccyx and scraping my hands on the cold

path. Tears fell down my cheeks, but they weren't from the pain. I slowly got to my feet and trudged down the path and out onto the street. I stopped and looked back at the house. A light was on in Finn's bedroom. There was a silhouette outlined in shadow. It was May. She was grinding up and down, her hands in her hair. She was only there for a moment, then a shadowy pair of hands pulled her roughly out of sight.

I threw up.

Nothing could have prepared me for this. They were dating, so it made sense. But... she'd kissed me. She had been about to... touch me. I was sure of it.
I thought about going to the den, but even in my distressed state I could tell that it wouldn't be safe; it was too dark. I sat down on the opposite side of the road to my pile of vomit and shivered until I saw my front door open. May stepped out, followed by Finn. I froze but realised that I'd only be seen if they were looking for me. I was scrawny and hunched as I was in my dark jacket under a broken street lamp, it was very unlikely I'd be spotted. They shared a cigarette, and then May left. No kiss goodbye. She turned the corner at the end of our road and melted into the darkness.
I checked my watch. 9:45. My parents would be back in fifteen minutes. I waited for another five in the cold, giving Finn enough time to get back to his room and light up another cigarette.

I didn't creep back inside. I hadn't exactly been stealthy when I left, so there seemed little point. Closing my bedroom door, I let out a deep breath and crouched in the middle of the floor. Crying was all I could do. Silent sobs broke in new waves each time I thought it was over.
My mother came to check on me when they got home, but I pretended to be asleep. I lay awake for hours, going over the whole evening's events in vivid detail. The anger and

hurt didn't dissipate, but one thought kept me from marching into Finn's room and strangling him: what would have happened if he hadn't come home?

My mind grew tired of the constant reruns, and I let it drift into dangerous territory. May's hand on my belt. My hot cheeks. Our lips touching. My heart started pounding again. I knew what was happening, but unlike earlier, I didn't care. My hand was shaking, but I placed it gently on the shaft of my penis and let my imagination run.
I saw her silhouette in the window, but I was there. Present. She was on me. I was in her. Her body was hot and heaving against mine. Pushing down and begging me to push up.
I was jolted back to the present by an intense rush inside me. I was ready, but the feeling passed. I was emotionally drained and too angry to feel anything else.
I sighed and rolled over. Something on my desk caught my eye. I hadn't noticed before, but there was a piece of folded paper on top of my math book. It hadn't been there earlier. I picked it up and something fell to the floor. I reached for the item but my eyes were drawn to the words inside the paper.

I'm sorry. I meant to break it off with Finn, I swear. But yanno what he's like. I can't get away. Sorry for what happened. Have to go or Finn will come looking.

A new wave of anger hit me and I screwed up the note and threw it across my room. Then I remembered the thing that had fallen. It was a picture. May and I standing outside the den. She was beaming and had her arms wrapped around my neck, and I stood awkwardly, half smiling. Hal had taken it last summer. On the back, May had written,
Sammy and me at the den. July, '61.
Then underneath, in what looked like newer ink,

Remember, I love you.
I gripped the image with white knuckles, but as I stared into her black and white face, my anger melted away and was replaced with the familiar sense of longing. She loves me, but she doesn't love me how I love her.

March, 1962

May and Finn had an on and off relationship for the next few months, though I never found out it had been off until it was back on again. Even then it wasn't lost on me how controlling my brother could be. I'd never seen him get violent towards May, but I knew he was capable of it. Regardless of her reasons for staying, it hurt. We never spoke about what had happened between us, so I left it alone.

A new diner opened in town, and Hal convinced me to ask Nancy's friend Lynn out for milkshakes. I agreed, but only if Hal promised to bring Nancy and make it a double date. He begrudgingly said yes, but only if I paid.

It was bitterly cold, but as Finn was the one with the car that night, I had to pick Lynn up on foot. Her house was near Hal's, in the rich part of town and, as I knocked on the door, I noticed 3 cars in the drive, one of which was a Bentley. I promised Lynn's father that I'd have her home by eleven, and then we walked quickly (due to my nerves, and only in part to the cold) to meet Hal and Nancy at the diner.

She was very shy and polite, and her demeanour was mirrored in her milky skin and pale pink dress with a matching sweater.

"So," I said, rubbing the back of my neck nervously. "I like that car back there. The black Bentley."

"Thanks," she replied, her voice sweet and quiet. "It's my father's pride and joy. He spends hours just sitting in it."

"He doesn't drive it?"

"He doesn't want to get it dirty!" We both laughed awkwardly. There was a long pause, in which I gave her my jacket. "Thanks. Nancy told me Hal takes her down to your den sometimes."

"Yeah, sometimes." We crossed the street and I could see the diner lights up ahead.

"I'd like to go there. Maybe you could take me one day?"
"Maybe."

We didn't speak again until we reached the diner door. I held it open for her and we found a cosy booth in the far corner. Hal and Nancy weren't here yet.
While Lynn studied the menu, I studied her. I'd always thought her plain, but out of a classroom or church setting, she was quite pretty. But every girl paled in comparison to May. I chided myself inwardly. I'm over May. I'm on a date with a nice girl. Stop it.

Lynn seemed a little like Nancy- innocent and sort of dull. They were both members of the chastity club and wore pins proclaiming this fact 24/7. But it wasn't like I was looking to do anything with her, so it didn't really bother me.
She ordered a strawberry milkshake that matched her dress, and I ordered a soda. Just as the drinks were brought to the table, I heard my name. I looked up, expecting to see Hal, but a waiter was coming toward me.
"Are you Sam?"
"Uh, yeah."
"Phone call. Behind the bar."
I excused myself and followed the waiter. I picked up the receiver and waited. Hal's voice crackled across the wire.
"Sam? Look I'm sorry but Nancy is real sick with the flu so we're not going to make it."
"Damn. Can't *you* come?"
"I would but my mom doesn't want me to go out. She thinks it might snow and because it's dark... well, you know how moms are."
"Are you sure you can't come?" I felt angry. I was sure he was lying.
"Yeah, I'm sorry Sam. You have a nice night with Lynn though."
"Uh-huh." I hung up the phone. As I walked back to the table I could feel my frustration bubbling up. I thought

we'd gotten past this. The only way he could help himself was to try. I bet Nancy wasn't even sick.

"Nancy has the flu," I said to Lynn. I hovered next to her, unsure whether this meant the date was over or not.

"Oh, that's too bad!" She sounded concerned but there was an unmissable twinkle in her eye. She paused for a moment and then said, "What do you say we get out of here?"

It took me by surprise. Her shyness had vanished. "Um...sure. Where do you wanna go?"

She took a final sip of her milkshake and smiled. "Guess!"

I racked my brains trying to think of somewhere, anywhere in town that she'd want to go. The only place I could think of was Frank's Bistro on Feldman Street, but only parents went there. "I dunno... I'd drive us somewhere but I don't have the car."

"I wanna see the den!" She linked arms with me and dragged me towards the door. I put some money down on the table and followed her, not sure how to refuse. My guard was up. It wasn't like I thought she'd... what? I didn't know. I just didn't want her near the den.

"Oh... um... it's getting kinda late." We were out on the street now and Lynn looked at me expectantly.

"It's only 9:30," she said, checking an expensive-looking watch. "C'mon Sam!"

"Uh... I dunno..."

She leaned in close to me. "I'll let ya kiss me."

I laughed nervously, guessing she was kidding around, but the way she placed her hand on my chest made me think she wasn't.

As much as I didn't want her to, May was invading my thoughts once more. But this time it was the image of her writhing against Finn's top-heavy body while I watched helplessly from the corner. She'd be jealous if I started dating Lynn. I knew she would. It wouldn't even have to be serious. Just a bit of fun.

"Okay."

We stopped off at my house on the way to get a couple of flashlights and a blanket, and for Lynn to use the restroom. In front of my parents, she was back to the meek girl I'd picked up at 8. All "goodness me Mrs Harvitz!" and "those drapes are perfectly lovely!"

Finn was nowhere to be seen. Presumably still out, stuffed full of drugs.

A few minutes later we waved goodbye to my mom and dad, and just as we stepped off the path I heard a familiar voice say, "Oh!".
My stomach flipped and I instantly wished the ground would swallow me up.
"Hey, Sam. I was just calling on your brother. Who's this?" May asked in a jovial tone.
Lynn stuck out her hand and May shook it. "I'm Lynn! Sam and I are on a date."
May laughed. "At home? C'mon Sam, think bigger! I'm May."
I didn't know what to say. I was still angry with her, but she didn't know that. "Well, no...we're about to go to the den actually. Finn's not here by the way."
"Oh." she sounded disappointed, but I couldn't tell if it was because of Finn, or my date. "If Finn's not here then I guess I'll go! You have a nice night." She winked at me and walked away. As she passed under a streetlight, I noticed that her hair was done up and she seemed to be wearing a new dress. Finn had stood her up. As upset as I was with her, I couldn't help feeling bad as her figure disappeared around the corner. I didn't like to think of her crying over my dipshit brother.
"She seems nice, but a bit... yanno," Lynn said carelessly as we walked.
"What d'ya mean?"
"I dunno, just... trashy."
I was taken aback, but let it slide. "Well yanno. She's older." is all I could think to say.

"Are you okay?" She put a hand on my arm.
"Yeah."

Once we reached the den, Lynn squealed and ran ahead. She stopped just outside the door and peered in with her flashlight. "It's kinda small," she said, poking the curtained doorway. "Look how moth-eaten this is!" she laughed lightheartedly, but I knew she wasn't impressed.

"It's really old," I said in defence. I held the curtain back for her and we shuffled inside, placing the flashlights across from us so we could see. We sat in silence for a while.

"So, you all come down here, every day?" Lynn turned so she was lying on her side, facing me.

"Most days, yeah. More in the summer."

"The way Nancy and Hal talk about it, I thought it'd be like a castle!" she laughed and played with her hair. I was pretty sure she was flirting with me. I didn't say anything, just smiled dryly and leaned back on my arms.

"There's a hole in the wall. Ya see?" she pointed at a tiny gap in the wood, barely bigger than her fingernail. I nodded. She was starting to piss me off.

"Maybe we should get back. It's school tomorrow and all."

"We only just got here! But I guess you're right. It's a little damp!" I held my tongue. "I'd like to come back though," she said.

I snapped. "You would, would you?" I didn't mean to be harsh, but she had continually insulted my haven since we arrived. She wriggled away from me and stared at me shocked. Her doe eyes brimmed with tears.

"Nah... Lynn, I'm sorry."

"What was that for? I was just saying..."

"I know," I interrupted her. I couldn't blame her. She had probably been expecting more. And I wasn't angry with her. Seeing May had thrown me off when I was already anxious about the date. "I'm sorry."

“It’s that girl isn’t it?” She moved close to me again. She’d obviously picked up on my awkwardness before. I shook my head but she put a hand on my cheek and drew my face close to hers. “Forget about her.” I thought she might kiss me, but she didn’t. She was in the chastity club after all.

I decided to fill the silence. “Finn and May have been together for a while and it just gets under my skin that she’s with my brother.” Lynn looked at me quizzically and I stammered a quick recovery. “No! Not because I *like* her or anything, Finn is just... an asshole. And she’s a friend so... I don’t want her to get hurt.” I mustn't have sounded very convincing, because Lynn let go of my face and sat back, sighing.
“You should try and get over her.”
“I’m not...”
“Uh-huh.” She crossed her arms and smiled, pulling a blue blanket around us both. Thankfully, that seemed to be the end of the conversation about May. She leant her head on my shoulder, and I realised I didn’t dislike her as much as I’d convinced myself I would. Now she’d come out of her shell, she had more substance to her and I could see us maybe going out again. I really did want to get over May.

“Do you wanna go out next Tuesday?” I asked. It was the first sincere thing I’d said all night.
“Sure! Maybe Nancy will be feeling better.”
“I thought maybe... just us.”
She looked at me coyly. “Oh really?”
“No, no that’s not what I me...” Lynn smashed her lips onto mine, pushing me to the floor. After a second of confusion and another deciding just how sure I was about getting over May, I gave in and kissed her back.
The rhythm changed every so often. Sometimes slow and seductive, then it would pick up frantically and we’d be panting for breath. She was straddling me now, her dress bunched up around her waist and she moved gently,

grinding up and down. She knew she was making me hard.
"I thought you were..." I gasped.
"The chastity club? I have to be. My best friend is the minister's daughter for god's sake!" She kissed me again and then stopped abruptly. "You've done this before, right?"
"Uh, yeah." I lied. "You?"
"A couple of times. My last boyfriend was someone from church and we only got as far as kissing, but the one before that... yeah. We did it a couple of times."

Sex. She meant sex. Did I want to have sex? Of course. I was 16. But did I want to do it now, with Lynn? To be honest, I did. I was certainly aroused- not necessarily by her, but by what she was doing. And the anger I felt towards May was burning me up inside. I needed it out. So, we did it. Probably for all the wrong reasons. But we did.

She slipped off her white underwear and I undid my belt and shimmed my pants down my legs. I had no idea what I was doing, but the first part seemed pretty self-explanatory.
I felt an instant rush of pleasure, but after a few moments, the up and down motion was numbing and the ecstasy I'd imagined was somewhat muted. Lynn was perfectly silent, as was I. No moans or exclamations. Just heavy breathing. A moth had come in through a gap in the curtains. It circled one of the flashlights, bumping into the bulb with a dull slap every few seconds. It felt like we'd been doing this for hours.
I shook myself back into the moment. Focus. This is an important moment. I cleared my throat. I was getting a cramp in my leg. Lynn stopped moving and I asked if we could change position. She agreed, and I rolled on top of her. The cramp eased. This was better. Not perfect, but better. The wind had picked up. Focus. I looked into Lynn's eyes, searching for any indication that this was anything

more than a cheap fling in the woods. Nothing. I was getting tired. She didn't meet my gaze.

My mind drifted once more. There she was. Lynn had melted away and May was staring up at me, smirking. A shudder went through my body and the pleasure I'd felt at the beginning came flooding back. I moaned and squeezed my eyes shut, willing the image to stay. I could feel something now. My speed picked up and Lynn let out a quiet noise. I ignored her, focusing all my energy on May. This was it. I gasped loudly and gripped the faded carpet as my whole body pulsed. Once, twice, and a third time. I collapsed on top of Lynn heavily as I finished. She remained silent.

I pulled out and instantly shielded my exposed half from her as if the intimacy we had just shared had never happened. She instinctively pulled her dress down and reached for her underwear. She didn't say anything, but she smiled at me dryly as she made herself presentable again. I wanted to ask her how it was, but her silence unnerved me. Maybe she'd hated it.

We exchanged only small talk as I walked her home. She seemed shy and sweet once more as if nothing had happened. On the corner of her road, she stopped and put her hand on my arm. "Am I your girl now?" she asked, looking at me expectantly.

"Sure," I said. Why not? Half of it was that I hoped our clandestine activity had driven a wedge between May and me and that it had given me the magical power to forget about her. But also, I wanted the opportunity to fuck again. I'd be able to use Lynn's silence to conjure May. There was the bonus of making May potentially jealous if she had cared about me as she claimed. Lynn put her arms around my neck and kissed me. I held her in the embrace for a moment and then walked her to the house.

I didn't feel like going straight home, so instead, I meandered my way back to the den. It wasn't far. I sat for a while, collecting my thoughts. The date had been a success by all accounts. I definitely enjoyed it more than anticipated. There was a niggling feeling in my chest, which I decided was May trying to worm her way back into my heart. I wouldn't let her. She'd hurt me more than anything ever could. I deserved to be happy, and if it wasn't with May, then so be it. Lynn was a lovely girl. Smart and pretty. I could do worse.

My shallowness never came from a place of indifference. I truly meant to fall in love with Lynn for her substance and soul, but it didn't seem to matter to me that much. In the end, I did love her. I do love her. I told her so when we got married.

May, 1962

"Are you sure?"

"Not totally but... I'm late."

I stood helplessly under the bleachers, leaning heavily against a post. Lynn sat down on the grass unceremoniously. "How can you find out for sure?" I asked, my hands shaking.

"I don't know." Lynn looked over her shoulder at Hal who was standing at the other end of the bleachers, pretending not to listen. He was the one who'd dragged me out of my Chem class under the pretence of a family emergency and rushed me out to the field. "I'll have to just wait and see. Does he have to stand there?" She gestured in Hal's direction.

"You're the one who told him."

"Who else was I supposed to tell?" She was angry. "My best friend is head of the chastity club. Believe me, I wouldn't have if I had any other option!"

I still found it strange. "I'm sorry." I sat down and put an arm around her. My heart was beating out of my chest and there was a fuzziness at the edge of my vision.

Pregnant.

That was something that happened to other people. She'd gotten her period in March, but then nothing. At first, I'd been relieved, but then I recalled another messy fumbling in the back of her Dad's Bentley in April and my heart sank. If she was indeed pregnant, would I step up? My instinct was to run for the hills, but my parents would never allow it. I'd marry Lynn and support her and the baby. Baby. It hadn't registered in my brain that pregnancy meant an actual physical human in the end.

"Next period."

My head snapped around. "Huh?"

Lynn looked at me, confused. "Next period just started. That was the bell."

I nodded numbly and kissed her stiffly goodbye. As she walked away I let out a loud groan. Hal wandered over and put a consoling hand on my shoulder. I looked at him and held my hands up in surrender. "Shit," I said. He nodded in agreement and held out his hand to help me up. My legs felt like lead. He asked me if I was going to the dance next month. I hadn't even thought about it.

"Lynn will want to go." He said, climbing out from underneath the bleachers and leading me to two seats in the middle row.

"I guess so. It's honestly the last thing on my mind right now Hal."

"You need to pretend everything is normal. That's what I do." He was probably right. I still felt slightly sick but I allowed myself to be drawn into the conversation.

"Will you take Nancy to the dance?" I asked. Hal shifted uneasily.

"No... we aren't... we broke up."

"When?"

"The night of the double date. She wasn't sick. I'd just been over to tell her I was calling it off." He picked at some mud on his shoe.

"I thought you said you were gonna try?"

"I did. It's nothing to do with... that. She's just got a lot on, and so have I. Exams and... yanno."

I wasn't in the mood to probe any deeper. My own problems seemed far more pressing. "Hey, thanks for missing class for me. I know you hate that."

He laughed sadly and patted my arm. "It's alright. It's only Shakespeare. I'm indifferent, really." His sarcasm was dripping and I laughed in spite of my mood. He chuckled too. I don't know how he managed to do it, but he always made everything seem okay. "We should probably get back." We picked up our bags and headed back to the building.

A thought struck me. "Hal, did Lynn say why she told you about all of this? She has plenty of friends. Not Nancy, obviously, but..."

"I assume she thought I'd keep her secret. Because of my loyalty to you."

I turned to face him. "She knows, doesn't she?" I lowered my voice. "About you and Desmond."

Hal coughed lightly. "We both have appearances to maintain." He turned to walk away. "Oh, Sam?"

"Yeah?"

"Next time, use a rubber." With that, he waved a stiff goodbye and marched back to class. My best friend was usually so cryptic, but this time I knew I was right. Lynn knew about Desmond.

July, 1962

Joe's birthday fell on the Saturday before the school dance. We all piled into the back of his pick-up truck and he drove us into Des Moines. Me, Hal, Finn and Joe had planned to go to the movies but there wasn't anything on so instead, we went down to Greenwood Park and drank scotch out of a rusty flask that Joe had brought. Lynn and May went off to see May's half-sister June as she was a seamstress. She'd made a dress for May and was altering the hem on Lynn's. She'd given me the number on a torn napkin in case they took too long, but we didn't mind because it gave us an excuse to smoke and watch city women in the park.

I'd been hesitant when May suggested taking Lynn with her. They'd gotten on fine when Lynn had joined us in the den, and I think she enjoyed having another girl to talk to, but her sister lived on the other side of town so it was a long journey for them to be alone together. I was worried Lynn might let it slip that we'd been having sex. Hal knew, but no one else did. Lynn hadn't liked May when they first met and because she suspected my crush, she would potentially tell all to make her jealous. I managed to convince myself that I was overthinking. The smoke helped. They barely knew each other, and with Lynn being pregnant... there's no way she'd want anyone to know yet.

The pregnancy was weighing heavily on my mind. It was now June, and with nothing to indicate we were in the clear, the cold hands of fatherhood were firmly around my neck. We'd discussed waiting until the end of the month before really starting to think about the future, but that didn't stop the dread.

After a couple of hours, Hal spotted May and Lynn walking toward us with dress bags draped over their arms. They were giggling with each other. It made me happy to see them getting along, but the closer friends they became, the harder it would be for me. As soon as they were within earshot they stopped talking and whispered behind their hands.

"What are you birds whispering about?" Finn said roughly. He took May by the waist and kissed her sloppily.

"Nothing, just the dance," May said, pushing him away. It seemed lighthearted but she winced.

I kissed Lynn on the mouth and we all stood and talked for a while. Joe was chatting up a pair of girls by the path and Hal stood next to him, looking intently down at his feet. I kept catching myself looking at May, and most notably her body. I assured myself this was okay because I looked at Lynn an equal amount. It wasn't a lost longing for May anymore. I just wanted women.

Over the past few weeks, I'd been studying Lynn's stomach and breasts to map any changes. If she was pregnant then it'd show there first. I remembered when my kindergarten teacher had gotten 'in trouble' and had to leave the school. Lynn didn't look any different today. She looked very beautiful. My feelings for her had certainly grown beyond amicable liking. It wasn't love. Not yet. But it was enough.

We stopped in a motel diner on the way back for hamburgers. About halfway through the meal, Lynn stood abruptly and made her way to the bathroom. After a few minutes without her return, May left to go and check on her. After another few minutes, she returned and spoke to Finn. "I need to borrow 10 bucks."

"What for?"

"I just need to. Please?"

"Make it worth my while." He stroked her arm and pulled himself up so he was standing behind her. She whispered something in his ear, to which he responded with a growl and pushed his crotch hard up against her. He fished out $4 and Hal subbed her the rest. She left the diner, came back a few minutes later with something under her jacket, and went into the bathroom. She returned with Lynn and we resumed the meal as normal.

I was confused. Lynn's long absence had worried me and May's secrecy surrounding the money had made it worse. On the way back to the truck I pulled Lynn to the side and asked if she was okay.

"Let's just say... I'm not pregnant." Relief flooded my veins.

"You... got... yanno... it?"

"I'm just... not pregnant." She said again. Something seemed off, but I was too thankful to press her further.

I can recall a similar occasion a few years later when I came home to find her sobbing on the kitchen floor. It was the second of her four miscarriages before we got lucky.

I smiled at May from across the sidewalk as we climbed into the truck, as thanks for helping Lynn. She looked at me but didn't smile back.

The Night

July 19th, 1962. I remember everything. It was the day before graduation and the night of the school dance.
I picked Lynn up in my Dad's car before the dance and we stopped to get Hal and Nancy on the way. He and Nancy weren't back together, but neither of them had a date so decided to couple up for the evening. Finn wasn't going. He'd bundled into the back of a friend's truck with six other guys and they'd gone whooping into town. This had left May without a date, so Joe stepped in and asked her. They were meeting us there. Finn hadn't been thrilled by it, but it hadn't bothered him enough to convince him to come.

The car ride was silent apart from the odd word or two between Lynn and Nancy. I kept thinking about how poofy their dresses were and what the best way would be to get access under Lynn's after the dance. Her dress was light blue and she'd picked out a matching tie for me. The dress stuck out awkwardly and covered half of the front of the car. Nancy's dress was causing similar issues in the back. It was the same style- they'd bought them together- but hers was a hideous shade of milky green. It looked like vomit. This made me feel a little smug. Nancy was arguably the most desirable girl in school, partly due to the fact that she wouldn't give *it* away, and yet tonight, my girl looked the best. Lynn really did look beautiful. She'd had her hair done and now she wasn't worried about being pregnant she seemed a lot happier. Hal and I had basic tuxes, but his was paired with a ruffled shirt and shoes that had been shined to within an inch of their lives.

The gym was heaving when we arrived. We handed in our tickets and the girls made an instant beeline to their friends to show off their dresses. I stood with Hal, our backs against the refreshments table.

"Do you think you'll start up again with Nancy?" I asked, offering him a glass of punch.
He pushed it away. "You know that's probably been spiked?" He didn't answer my question.
"What makes you say that?" I asked inquisitively. He gestured across the ridiculously over-decorated gym to a group of guys a few years older. Joe was there. He'd been watching us, amused. He stuck his hands up in surrender and I saw a flask in his left hand. "Ah." Hal and I laughed stiffly. I took a sip anyway and tasted both orange and paint thinner. "Vodka."

Lynn was by my side. She asked me to dance and I obliged. We danced to a few songs on the outskirts of the hall. Every time I spun Lynn around to the beat, I caught May's gaze. She looked lonely, sitting there on the bleachers. Joe was talking with his friends. I don't think he had asked her to dance. I had another glass of punch and brought some to Lynn that came from the reserve bowl under the table. I hoped Joe hadn't found that one. Around 9:15, Lynn said she needed some air, so we went out into the parking lot. I was slightly drunk and high on the atmosphere, so I hadn't wanted to leave, but I knew that if I agreed I'd probably get under that dress.

We sat on the hood of the car and looked up at the sky. The sun had just set so it wasn't quite dark. A milky blue haze hung on everything so there were no stars, but I still felt content. Better than I'd felt in a long time. Lynn rested her head on my shoulder and I kissed her forehead lightly. She looked up at me with her doe eyes and smiled. I could sense she wanted to say something, but she didn't open her mouth. I cupped her face in my hands and kissed her. She kissed me back and soon we were making out under the sky. Someone came out into the parking lot, yelling and shouting about something. I pulled Lynn off the car and into the back seat so we wouldn't be seen. She giggled and I reached a hand under her skirt. I played there for a while, touching what I found and making mental notes to return to the places that made her squirm. We had to be quiet in the car, but that added to the fun. She unzipped my fly and kissed me everywhere, then settled down to business until I was gripping the seat to contain myself. This was a routine we were comfortable with. We didn't have penetrative sex very often as I could only get rubbers by sneaking one from Finn's draw and I didn't want him to notice.

After, we lay on the seats for a while. We talked about school and plans for after graduation. I was going to go and work for my Uncle's company in Chicago as an office assistant. Lynn was staying in town. We'd talked a little about what it meant for us, but not seriously. I'd assumed we'd do what everyone else did. Get married. But something was stopping me from asking her. I couldn't put my finger on it, but there was always a lump in my throat when I thought about it.

I sat up slowly, and wiping off the condensation, peered out of the window. The lot was empty. "We should probably go back in. Hal and Nancy will wonder where we are." Lynn nodded, but just as I was about to open the door, there was a loud clang on the side of the car. "The fuck?" I stopped and wiped the window again to see what had hit us. I couldn't see anything... wait! There was something... someone moving between the hedges in front of the car.

"Maybe it was a fox?" Lynn proffered. I shh-ed her and looked harder. It was definitely two people.

"I think it's a couple fooling around," I said, sighing. "Let's go." We clambered out and tried to look innocent as we smoothed out our clothes and ran fingers through our hair. A truck pulled up and Finn and his friends piled out noisily. Guess they'd decided to show up after all. We hung back to let them go in.

"Where's my purse?" Lynn said suddenly.

"Dunno."

"I need it, it has my compact in it."
I rolled my eyes. "Check the back seat. I'll see if you left it on the hood." I walked around to the front of the car and bent down to check under it. A rustling came from the hedges and I heard a male voice talking in whispers. It was very dark now so I found a stick lying nearby and used it to check underneath the car. The purse wasn't there. I was about to stand up when I noticed something out of the corner of my eye. In my crouched position I could see under the neatly trimmed hedges. I could see shoes. Very shiny shoes, even in the dark. A glimmer of recognition flashed across my mind but soon fled. I heard voices again. Then Lynn appeared.
"I've got it." She brandished her purse. The whispering stopped abruptly, but not before I thought I'd caught my name being bandied about in the dark.

"Hello?" I said into the gloom, walking closer. I turned to Lynn. "Maybe they were spying on us?" I said, annoyance and embarrassment flushing my cheeks red. The lone streetlamp cast a dim light but it was bright enough for me to discern two shapes among the foliage.
"Just leave it," Lynn said, taking my hand. "Probably Marcie and John. She told me earlier that he wanted to..."
"Yeah." I sighed. We hadn't gotten more than two yards away when I heard them again. I stopped. Snippets of a voice I knew.
"Certain... was Sam. Shhh... He's gone."
Abruptly, I let go of Lynn's arm and told her I'd meet her inside. I marched towards the bushes and pushed my way through.

Fuck.

I wish I could take it back. I wish I'd listened to Lynn and left it alone. I wish it didn't matter.
Desmond Hargreaves quickly pulled up his pants and shot off into the night. Hal was frozen in horror, kneeling on the

damp grass. His shirt was undone and his eyes shone with desperate tears as he lifted his head to look at me.

My heart was beating loudly in my ears. The only sound was my blood pumping and Hal's rapid breathing. My mind raced with possibilities. What should I do? It would be easy enough to walk away. Pretend it was nothing. Tell Lynn I'd seen Marcie and John passionately fucking against a tree. But he was my best friend. He'd lied to me. He had looked me in the eye and sworn. It wasn't really anger at what he'd done. It was the lie.

The unlearning took me years. It took me until my son's 20th birthday when he brought home his boyfriend Stuart for dinner. My son was still my son, and I loved him even more now that he was happy and he could let me in.

But in 1962, I kicked Hal 7 times. Anger boiled over and all I could see was red. Twice in the stomach, once on the leg as he fell to the ground, and then four times wherever my feet fell. I bloodied his nose, though I don't think it was broken. He never made a sound. He accepted all of it as if this was expected. Deserved.

With surprising strength, I pulled up him to his feet by his collar and pushed him against the hard tree trunk behind. My face was close enough to his that I could count the freckles on his blood-caked nose.
"You liar! You fucking liar!" I snarled through gritted teeth. I wanted to smash his head hard against the tree. I could have killed him.
"I'm sorry." He said. He didn't sound hurt or angry. He sounded tired. That pissed me off even more.
"You're sorry? Huh?" I pushed my arm hard against his chest, stopping him from escaping- not that he tried. "You swore *he* was a mistake. You promised. What about Nancy? Huh? Did you ever think about her? No! You just wanted *him*! You pervert." I spat in his face, and a single tear

tipped over from his eye to his cheek, creating a pink runway through the blood.

A gasp from behind. I whirled around and saw Lynn, clasping her hand to her mouth.
"Lynn, go back inside," I said forcefully. She didn't move. "GO!" She knew. I could see it in her face. Pity mixed with fear and confusion. "Go inside. Now." I dropped Hal and he crumpled to the floor. Grabbing Lynn by the arm, I pushed her towards the school.
"Sam, wait..." She started to speak, but I put a firm hand over her mouth. Her frightened eyes darted to the left. Nancy was standing next to us, wide-eyed. I watched her face as she took in the scene. She'd obviously heard everything. Panic set in. I lowered my hand from Lynn's mouth in slow motion and put my hands up in surrender, begging them both.
"Nancy... please go back to the dance." She shook her head. "Okay... I can take you home if you want." She wasn't listening, just staring at Hal, hatred burning in her eyes. He seemed to feel her gaze gouging holes in his head because he looked up. They locked eyes.
"How could you?" She said quietly.
Hal rose to his feet with great effort.

"I love him." It was the most sincere thing he had said in years.

Nancy burst into tears and ran back towards the school. Lynn took off after her. I looked at Hal for a moment. The immediate anger was fading.
"You need to leave," I said. He nodded and quietly buttoned up his grass-stained shirt. I knew he loathed the mess. "I'll go and get the girls. Before anyone asks questions." I said. He looked as though he might say something, but no words came. He limped away into the night, his head bent low.

I intended to make good on my word and find the girls, but I was shaking uncontrollably. I walked slowly towards the car and smoked a cigarette as I cried into my arm. I wasn't sure how long I did this, but after a while, I pulled myself together.

People had started to filter out into the parking lot. I pushed through a crowd of happy teens and ran into the gym. There were only two dozen or so people left, kicking around streamers and finishing their punch. Lynn and Nancy were nowhere to be found. I spun around anxiously, scanning the faces of those nearby. The band was packing up so I pulled myself onto the stage for a better look. Something above caught my eye. The gymnasium doubled as an auditorium and there was a small gallery containing a projection room that overlooked the floor. A shadowy figure was leaning against the barrier. I could see the outline of a dress. She must have noticed me looking, as she moved away from the edge and into obscurity. Lynn maybe? I couldn't see well enough.

Making sure none of the teachers saw me, I went out through the fire escape and climbed the rickety stairs up to the gallery. I pushed open the heavy door at the top with a whoosh and stepped out onto the balcony. It was freezing. The gym was enormous so the heating didn't reach up here.

"Lynn?" I said into the near darkness.

"Guess again." A disembodied voice replied. She stepped out from the gloom.

"Oh... May." Hal, Lynn, Nancy. They all fell out of my mind the second I saw her.

"You could sound a little more enthusiastic." She said it dryly, but I knew her well enough to know her eyes would be sparkling with mirth.

"What are you doing up here? It's fuckin' freezing."

"It was too hot down there. Besides, there's nothing else to do."

"Where's Joe?" I asked. She took a few steps toward me. I could see her face now. There were no tear tracks in her makeup, but something told me she'd been crying. Her dress, bright pink and navy, was crumpled at the bottom.
"Finn came in and started yelling at him for bringing me. I told Joe to leave before they started throwing punches." She peered over the gallery. "Well... if I need to get home, Finn can take me. Have you seen him?"
Annoyance flashed over my face. I hoped it was too dark for her to see. "Uh, no. Not since he arrived."
She turned towards me with surprise. "He's not downstairs?" I shook my head. She scoffed. "She must have said yes then."
"Who? To what?"
"About 10 minutes ago, Lynn and Nancy came back in. Nancy was sobbing and Lynn was trying to comfort her but she was crying so loudly everyone was staring. I went over and took them to one side, but neither would tell me what the hell was going on." I inwardly breathed a sigh of relief. "I know Nancy doesn't like me but Lynn..." She looked at me pointedly. "Anyway. Joe had left and Finn had no one to maim so he came over. Offered to drive them both home in that truck. He only did it to make me jealous, so I left them. Didn't think they'd say yes."
Anxiety filled my chest. "You let them go with him?"
"I didn't want to." She was suddenly defensive. "I tried to say something. He wouldn't *do* anything."
She was right. My brother was brutish and cruel, but he would never do anything that might get him in serious trouble. It was all for show. I hoped.
"Yeah. He's not that kind of guy." I said. Despite my conviction that all Finn would do is drive them home and probably try his luck for a goodnight kiss, I still felt uneasy. The evening had been full of the unexpected. Anything could happen.

"I need to speak to Lynn."
"Why?" She put a hand on my arm. "Is everything okay?"

I wanted to tell her. I would have given anything to yell "No!" and collapse into her arms so she could make it better. But I didn't. Our relationship hadn't been the same for a while now. I didn't trust her anymore.
"It's fine," I shrugged her off lightly. "I just need to speak with her as soon as possible." She could probably tell I was hiding something, but she took my hand and we went back down the stairs.
"We'll go to the phone booth on the corner. You'll be able to talk to her. Don't worry sweetie!" She said, winking as we got into the car. "Ah! To be young and in love!" She said, batting her eyelashes and pretending to faint. I laughed, in spite of my mood.

I pulled up to the phone booth and hastily opened the door. May stayed in the car, her hands clasped in her lap like she was at prayer. I fished a couple of coins out of my pocket and pushed them into the slot. I dropped one and cursed as it bounced off my shoe and rolled out of sight into a pile of mud and leaves. Punching in Lynn's number, I turned slightly so I could see May. She was watching a cat on the other side of the street with disinterest. My heart was beating very fast. The receiver emitted a low hum as I waited for the dial tone. It beeped, then rang for a few seconds, before a crackly voice said, "Hello?"
I realised I'd been holding my breath. "Hi, uh... is Lynn there?"
"Who is this? Do you know what time it is?" It was Lynn's father. His gravelly, angry voice was unmistakable.
"Oh... um... It's Sam. Samuel Harvitz." Mr Brady huffed a small sigh, and then I heard rustling and he said something away from the speaker. I heard a female voice getting louder and soon Lynn was in my ear.

"Hey, I'm sorry for leaving like that. Nancy wanted to get home and, well... I couldn't find you."
"You're okay?"

"I'm fine, why?" I asked what had happened with Finn and she replied, confused. "Nothing. He and Nancy flirted a bit. I think he was trying to cheer her up. He told her to forget about Hal..."
I interrupted her. "Did she tell him? Did she tell Finn?" I asked.
Lynn went quiet. "Not while I was in the car... but he dropped me off first. Then took Nancy home. I'm sorry. I don't know."
The phone beeped angrily at me. "Look, my time is running out but I need you to ask Nancy, okay? Call her, then call me at home." She agreed, and the line went dead. I sighed and put the receiver heavily back on the hook.

May and I drove home in silence, but once I pulled up outside my house we both went to speak at the same time. We laughed awkwardly and she gestured for me to speak first.
"Do ya want a lift home?"
She shook her head. "It's only a block away. I like to walk at night. It calms me." She got out and walked away. I sat for a few seconds with my hands on the wheel. I looked in my mirror and saw her shape heading off into the night. On impulse, I leapt out of the car and called down the street.
"May?" She turned expectantly. I suddenly realised I had no idea what I wanted to say. I fumbled around for the words but nothing important came. "Uh... thanks for thinking of the phone booth. Never would have thought of it."
She smiled. "No problem. Oh... Joe said we might be going down to the den later. Around midnight. If you wanted to come."
"Oh yeah, I'll try." We said goodnight again and I turned to go inside to wait for Lynn's call. As I approached the door, my father opened it.
"Son, I have a message for you from Lynn." I looked at him, panic swelling in my chest. "She told me to tell you that she was sorry, but she spoke to Nancy. I don't know what she

means but..." He noticed my forlorn expression. "Everything alright son?"
"Yeah fine." I made a split-second decision. "I have to go out."
"What? You only just got in!"
"Yeah, I know. It's nothing, I just... I left something at the dance." With that, I raced back to the car and jumped into the driver's seat. My heart was pounding and I had no idea where I was going to go, but I needed to get away.

Images of Hal being attacked by Finn kept flashing across my mind. They made me lose focus on the road more than once. I gripped the wheel so tightly that my knuckles went white. I was angry with Hal, but there was a growing sense of guilt in my gut. I'd hurt him. Badly. If his nose wasn't broken, it would be bruised for weeks. And what's more, we'd never fought physically before. My anger had scared me. I expected violence from Finn, but I never considered that his explosiveness could manifest in me too.
What I'd caught Hal doing wasn't the problem anymore. Back then, it made me uncomfortable and confused, but deep down, all I wanted was to see my best friend happy.

I turned a few corners blindly, choosing my direction based on where I felt like turning. I'd been around the outskirts of town at least three times by that point when I came to the main crossroads. There were no other cars about so I stopped in the middle of the street. Turning right would take me down Ambrose Street and lead back around to my block. Left would lead me out of town. I knew instantly where I needed to go. Turning left, I breathed a slow sigh and tried to calm my heart. About 2 minutes later, I pulled up to a dark track winding away from the road. I had to go to the den.

I knew there'd be a flashlight in the trunk- something I kept for when Lynn and I messed around in the back of the car. It was freezing by now and the wind had picked up, so

I also took my suit jacket that was lying across the back seat. I switched the flashlight on and started my pilgrimage down to the den. Truth be told, I didn't need the flashlight. I'd walked this path thousands of times and knew where every pothole was and when to walk on the right to avoid the fallen tree. I could see the path veering down the slope ahead. Nearly there. I needed to sit and think for a while. Somewhere I was safe.

As I approached, I heard voices. Rounding a large tree, I saw light coming from inside the den. I suddenly remembered what May had said. She was going to be there with Joe at midnight. I didn't have my watch on, so I assumed it must have been late already. I considered turning around. Ideally, I would have been alone to collect my thoughts, but I knew that they'd be able to cheer me up. With the light from inside, it was bright enough for me to see the door so I turned off my flashlight. I could hear May talking, but I couldn't make out what she was saying thanks to the wind.

I was about to step closer and reach for the curtain when May said, "I didn't think he'd react like that. I'm so sorry."

Something deep inside me made me hesitate and my hand paused a few centimetres from the fabric.

"I don't blame him. It's my fault." That wasn't Joe. The voice wasn't deep enough. "I'd have hit me too." It was Hal. What was he doing here?

I considered walking quietly away into the night. He wouldn't want to see me, and I didn't want to see him, but I couldn't tear myself away. I waited anxiously, my breath coming out in short, shallow gasps.

There were a few moments of silence followed by shuffling sounds and then Hal spoke again, louder this time. "I want it to go away. I don't know what to do." There was a desperation to his voice. I moved stealthily around the side of the den, careful not to make a sound. There was a knothole on the third plank in on the left, and I pushed my eye up to it so I could see. May was sitting near the door. She had changed out of her dress into navy slacks and a thick cream jumper. Hal sat to the side of her, his face partially obscured by the shadow from a lantern. He was still wearing his stained shirt. He looked awful. My heart sank as I realised that his state was all my fault.

"I'm glad you came and found me. You shouldn't be alone Sweetie. You're *not* alone." May said, putting a gentle hand over his.

"You don't hate me?" Hal looked up, hope glittering in his tearful eyes.

May seemed to choke back a sob. "Of course not. I love you with all my heart."

"Sam does. He hates me." Hal's face crumpled and he let out a loud cry, burying his face in his hands. May didn't say anything, just pulled him into an embrace and held him. She cried silently, and so did I. I sat on the cold ground and sobbed into the jacket sleeves. It broke my heart to hear him so defeated, despite everything.

After a few minutes, Hal went from crying to quietly sniffing, and I took this as my cue to dry my eyes too. I positioned myself again so I could see in. Hal looked up from his lap and stared at May. His eyes filled with tears again as he spoke. "I need it to go away. How I feel. Who I..." He grasped May's hands earnestly. "Please. Help me."

She looked at him with a puzzled expression. "I don't understand." She whispered.

"We could get married. After graduation. I'm going to college and I have a job lined up at my Grandfather's firm. You could see other men. Do whatever you want. But you could help me beat this thing. We could have children. You could cure me." He spoke as if he was in a frenzy, tripping over his words and practically shouting. I couldn't believe what he was saying, and obviously, neither could May. She shook her head as he clawed at her arms.

"We can't Hal! We'd never be happy. You know it doesn't work like that!"

With sudden speed, he grabbed her face with both hands and kissed her hard on the mouth. She instantly pushed him away. A loud gasp escaped from my mouth before I could stop it and May's head snapped in my direction. Hal didn't notice, he was too busy apologising. May and I made definite eye contact before I threw myself backwards from the wall and scrambled back into the dark wilderness. I stood shakily behind a tree- the tree May had appeared from behind years earlier.

I couldn't see them, but I knew they had come outside as the lantern light was flickering a few yards away. There were footsteps getting closer. I prayed that May hadn't realised it was me, but that was a foolish hope. We'd played 'Guess Who?' through that hole hundreds of times.
May spoke behind me. "Sam, I know you're there." Shit. I didn't have another option, so I sheepishly emerged from behind the tree and faced her. She was alone.
Seemingly aware of my confusion she said, "He's inside. I told him I needed some air."
I stood awkwardly, not knowing what to do. "I should probably just go..." I said, starting to walk away.
"Oh no you don't." She stepped in my way. I'd never seen her like this. Her eyes were glassy but there was an angry fire burning behind them. "You need to talk to him."
My defences went up. I scoffed. "Why would I want to do that?"
"He's your best friend, Sam. He fucked up by not telling you, that's all. Everyone fucks up. You can act like a jerk all you want, but I know you're not that guy. You care. Otherwise, you wouldn't be hiding in the trees. You can't understand the pain of loving someone you can't have. You're just a boy."
"What?" I turned on her, my face close to hers. All the anger and pain of the night and countless years spent

longing for her condensed into one ball of fury. "*I* don't understand?" Spit landed on her face. She stayed defiantly silent. "That's what I thought. You're full of shit. I have nothing to say to him." I was shouting, but only so the volume would drown out my uncertainty. I had been disgusted with Hal, but my initial anger had faded into a gnawing sense of guilt. May's self-righteous silence was grating on me. She always had to be right. There was a condescending gleam to her arched brows that made me want to scream. I did know the pain of loving someone I couldn't have. I'd known for years. "Yeah, actually, you're right. Everyone fucks up. You'd know all about that."

Her arrogant expression faltered. "What's that supposed to mean?"

"You know exactly what I mean. Or do you think fucking my brother and leading me on was a good idea?" My cheeks burned. I instantly regretted saying anything. I didn't want her to know the pain she'd caused me by being with Finn. I'd convinced myself that I'd moved on. I mellowed a bit. "Look, I'm sorry for hitting him, okay? I'm gonna go. Tell him I'm sorry."

She looked at me bitterly with tears in her eyes. "Tell him yourself." She motioned over my shoulder. I turned to see Hal standing upright in the doorway. He was shrouded in darkness as May had the lantern. I turned on my flashlight and shone it in his direction. He smiled sadly.

"What a night, huh?"

The three of us sat for a while on the scratchy rug, sharing a bottle of whiskey I found under a stool. May told me that Hal had turned up at her house covered in blood but they'd had to go down to the den to talk because her Aunt was home. They called in on Joe on the way and she told him not to come.

Hal explained that he was sorry that I'd seen what I had. I said it was fine, but there was an uncomfortableness to my words that was tangible. He apologised to May for asking so much of her, and for kissing her. She said that she understood.

I said I was sorry for hurting him. He said he forgave me, and I really think he meant it.

Then Hal stood up and said he should go, so I walked outside with him. The air was biting, and the wind gave a solemn soundtrack to our otherwise silent journey up the bank. Once we reached the path, Hal spoke.

"I'd understand if you didn't want to, but my parents are having a dinner party tomorrow night. A graduation celebration, I suppose."

"Oh," I hesitated. "I dunno. My parents were gonna take me out for pizza."

"Well... if not, then..." He smiled shyly. "They're welcome too, of course."

"Thanks." I thought about hugging him but went for a handshake. "Here," I handed him my flashlight and told him to put it under my car when he reached the road. "Just in case."

"Thanks. See you at graduation." He said.

I went back inside the den and sat down heavily. It was only then that I realised how tired I was. My knuckles ached and I was freezing. I pulled out two blankets and handed one to May who was hovering in the doorway. She sat close and we chatted about meaningless stuff for a while. It must have been way past midnight, but I didn't care. I'd deal with my mother's wrath later.

There was a lull in the conversation. "I'm sorry for shouting at you," I said. "I was angry. Not tryina excuse it but... I was mad."

"S'okay sweetie. So was I. I know what it's like to feel lost like that." She touched her face gently, wiping away a speck of mud. "Passed around family and friends with no proper home. It hurts. When Hal came to me tonight, I recognised the pain of rejection in his eyes." A tear rolled down her cheek and I instinctively reached over and wiped it away.

She pressed my hand into her cheek and kissed it softly, more tears falling from her tired eyes. Pulling my hand over her mouth, she started to cry. Her whole body shook with sadness, small gasps of air escaping between my fingers. I wrapped my other arm tight around her shoulders and pulled her in close, holding her into my chest. I hated seeing her like that. She was always so in control. Her vulnerability scared me and I wanted to wrap her up and protect her from everything. I knew I was the only person in the whole world that could keep her safe. I loved her. So much that it hurt. We hadn't always had the easiest relationship, but thinking about my life without her made me want to die. I couldn't breathe without her. She had stopped sobbing and was staring up at me.

"What?" She smiled, her wet face glinting in the low light.
"I love you." I pulled her up into a sitting position and grasped her face with my hands. I wasn't afraid. I'd never felt more sure. "I love you, May. I always have."
I kissed her then. It was forceful but soft. We'd kissed before, but the tenderness of the moment was so easily lost. I didn't want to cloud my love with lust. She needed to understand that I valued her for more than that. I wasn't Finn. Or Joe. At that moment I knew I could give her everything. Life with her was the only way that made sense. She kissed me back and let me absorb her body into mine as we sat entwined on the rug.
I felt her cold skin and smelt the summer night in her hair, and her hands felt like fire as they wandered all over me. She undressed and lay under the blanket and I joined her, pressing my body into her back, kissing her neck and gripping her thighs. She was so beautiful. She didn't try to hide from me and let me see her completely. I reached across her stomach and down between her legs where I felt wetness and warmth and brought her to orgasm before kissing her again and entering.

She was the only person that mattered. Everything else melted away and her face was centred in my vision. It was more than sex. I felt her love for me over all else, and when we orgasmed together, I stayed there, feeling her body wrapped around mine.
She choked back a sob and I was afraid I'd hurt her, but she pulled me into her arms and whispered,
"I love you too."

There have been many times over the years that I've questioned whether she meant it. I believe she loved me, and the life I'd pictured with her may well have happened if it weren't for the pain of what came next. I expected her to heal and she never did, which proved that in the end, I couldn't give her everything.

It comes in snippets. Single moments of noise and colour interspersed with the quiet sound of heavy breathing through the trees.

Once we were dressed, we sat by the river, May's head on my shoulder. We sipped at a stray bottle of whiskey, trying in vain to make it warm us. May brought up Lynn. It was the first time I'd thought about her since arriving at the den. I expected a pang of guilt to shoot through my chest, but nothing happened.
"I don't think you should tell her about this yanno." She said, tucking her hair behind her ears.
"Wasn't planning on it." We both laughed dryly. "When I break it off with her I won't say why."
"What do you mean?" She asked, handing me the bottle.
I took a long sip. "Maybe I'll tell her it won't work long distance."
"You can't end things with her Sam." She had a very serious look on her face. I was about to ask why, when she motioned for me to be quiet. "I love you sweetie, and I'm sure I always will, but you and I could never work in the real world."

Panic started bubbling in my heart. “What d'ya mean? Of course we would! We can save up and get a house and...”
“Sam... your job after graduation will take you out of the state. Who knows where you’d end up? You have prospects and a future. And I’m meant to be with someone... like your brother. We’d never escape it. You know that, deep down.”

I felt sick. She was right, but I wouldn’t admit it. “Please. Please May. We could do it. Let’s move anywhere. Anywhere but here. I want to be with you. You could come with me.”
“And do what? All I can do is work with my sister sewing dresses.”
I knelt next to her, begging her to understand. “Please May, just think about it. You love me, right?” She nodded. “Just think about it. We can get out of here.” I kissed her hard, and she pulled me into an embrace.
“I’m sorry Sam.”
My heart dropped but I could still hear it pounding in my ears. I gripped her arm tightly but she brushed me off and stood. I jumped up and held her shoulders so she had to face me. “May... don’t do this.” I kissed her again and she kissed me back, both of us crying and pressing against each other. “Please,” I whispered in her ear. She gazed into my eyes and I sensed she was going to give in.

“Hey!” A harsh shout ripped through the silence of the forest. May pushed me away and whirled around. “What the fuck are you doing?” Finn appeared from behind the den, Charlie, Robert and some other football players following behind. “Joe said I’d find you here. Fuck you. She’s mine.” He marched forward and grabbed May by the arm, twisting it so she cried out in pain.

“Don’t touch her!” I said, trying to loosen his grip. He laughed at me and with his other hand, pushed me into the dirt. The burning anger I’d felt earlier tonight reared up. I

wasn't going to let him hurt her again. I shot up off the ground and pushed my brother hard in the chest. It took him by surprise, and he stumbled, releasing May from his grasp. I advanced on Finn, my fists balled and ready.
"Sam, please don't!" May pleaded, trying to pull me back. "I'll go with him now and we can talk about this tomorrow, okay?" I shrugged her off. "Sam! I'm not going to let you get killed trying to save me. I can look after myself!" She was angry but I ignored her. Finn had taken her from me over and over and I couldn't let it go. He'd regained his balance and was smirking as I came closer.

"She doesn't want to be with you anymore," I said, a quiver in my voice. I was terrified.
"You think she wants to be with you?" He was playing with me.
"Yeah." We were centimetres away from each other. He grabbed me by the collar and held me up. His eyes were shining and almost completely black.
"You're fucking delusional. Do you think just because she fucked you, that that means something? If it was like that, she'd be dating all the guys here." He snarled, gesturing to his friends. I screamed with anger and kicked him in the leg. He threw me to the ground and jumped on top of me, pushing my face into the dusty ground. Coughing and choking on dirt, I tried to bring my fists down on his head but he just laughed.
"You're gonna pay, Sammy," Finn said, his voice dripping with condescension. May started towards me but Finn growled at her. "Don't you fucking move." She walked slowly towards him and put a hand on his chest.
"Come on Finn. Let me send him home... then I'll do anything you want, okay?" She ran her hand desperately over his crotch, but I could see fear in her eyes. She was trying to stop me from getting hurt but her touching my brother again made me want to scream. He suddenly let me go and May pulled me to my feet.
"Go. Sam, go!" She said, pushing me back towards the den.

"No! You can't stay with him!"
"I have to. Please, we'll talk tomorrow."
"I'll kill him," I said, turning back to the gang before me.
"What good will that do?" She said. "Please sweetie. Go home."

She was right. Trying to inflict any damage on Finn was a waste of time. If he wasn't already huge, he had backup. There was still no way I was going to leave her. I'd seen his eyes. He was high.
Finn and his friends were all laughing and teasing me. He was egging them on and motioning thrusts at May. I glared at him and he roared with laughter. "Fuck off Sam. Your faggot friend will give you anything *she* can't."
Rage raced through my veins. Enough. I'd had enough of my brother and his destruction. He deserved pain and I was the one who was going to give it to him.
"Don't you fucking talk about Hal." I rushed at him before May could stop me and pushed him over. I let off punch after punch and scratched and kicked and bit until I tasted blood. When they saw that Finn was having trouble fighting me off, Charlie, Robert and Billy stopped jeering and ripped me away, trapping me between their huge arms. Finn got up and spat a mouthful of blood onto the ground. It instantly curdled in the dirt. I was screaming and yelling at him, calling him any foul name I could think of. For the first time in his life, Finn was calm. He limped over and smiled at me.

"I could kill ya. But you're not worth it." He spat in my face. "Hold him." He said to Charlie.

They made me watch. Even when I tried to close my eyes, another thug held them open.
Finn grabbed May by the waist and yanked her feet off the ground. She yelped and tried to push him off. I heard her say he was hurting her, but he didn't care. "You said you'd do anything. So that's what you're gonna fucking do." He

said, cruel delight in his voice. May whimpered and struggled in his arms but she wasn't strong enough. I screamed for her, begging Charlie and Robert to let me go. Finn pinned her to the floor and ripped her trousers as he tore them off. She clawed at the earth, reaching out for me. She howled my name like a tortured animal as he raped her. The second time, he made his friends keep me on the ground next to her, close enough for our fingers to touch. One of the others tried to do it after, but Finn punched him. He picked up May's limp body with ironic tenderness and walked away into the darkness. The last thing I remember before blacking out was seeing the ghostly figure of long-dead Kevin waving as the colour faded from my vision.

The Day After

When I came to it was still dark. I couldn't have been out for longer than a few minutes or I would have frozen to death. I stood, still half-delirious, and stumbled along the path. The car was gone. Finn must have taken it. The flashlight was still there. I walked home in a state of shock. The car wasn't in the driveway either so I assumed Finn hadn't come home. My parents were asleep but I didn't go upstairs to bed. I sat down on the couch and stayed there until the sun came up. I was yelled at by my mother as my father looked on disappointedly. I told them I didn't know where Finn was. We'd fought and he'd driven off. That was it. I told my mom that I was sick and wasn't going to graduation but she made me shower and get dressed anyway. I wanted desperately to see if May was alright. Of course, I knew she wouldn't be, but I didn't know what else to do.

I left for school early so that I could stop at her place. No one answered the door and a neighbour who was collecting their newspaper told me that they'd seen May and her Aunt packing up the car early that morning and that they'd been gone by 7 am.

I drove frantically to the phone booth. There was only one other person May had in the world. Her sister in the city. I scrambled around in the glove compartment for the napkin with June's number on it and hastily jumped out to dial.

A woman answered and at first, I thought it was May, but she didn't recognise my voice. "June?"

"Uh... hello? Who is this?" May's sister sounded exactly like her.

"It's Sam."

"I don't know a Sam." She sounded impatient.

"No, I'm looking for May."

"She isn't here."

"She is." I pushed. "I know she is." There was silence for a moment and then June sighed.

"Alright."

A few moments later the rhythm of the line changed and I knew May was there.

"May..." I didn't know what to say. She didn't say anything either. "How long are you staying with your sister?"

"I don't know. I have to go and unpack."

"May, talk to me," I said, gripping the phone.

"What's there to say?"

I sighed. "I think we should tell someone... the cops maybe?"

She laughed bitterly. "No point. I told my aunt when I got home, but we both knew it'd make no difference."

"Why?" I cleared my throat to push back the tears.

"He's a guy, Sam. I don't want the hassle of disbelief." I tried to protest but she didn't let me finish. "It's easier if I stay here for a while... So I can move on."

"Move on?"

"Yeah... From all of it."

"Okay, well, can I come and see you?" The tears were hiding just behind my eyes, ready to explode at any moment. May was silent for a beat.

"I don't think that's a good idea sweetie. After I've sorted some things, I'm getting a place of my own out of state." The tears fell onto my cheeks but I wiped them away furiously.

"Why?" My voice was almost a whisper.

Her voice cracked slightly. "It's too painful Sam. When I think of us together it'll just remind me of him."

"That will change!" I was desperate. "It'll change with time!"

"It won't."

It occurred to me how much of the last few years May had spent at the mercy of my brother. As much as I wanted to believe her pain would go away, I knew it wouldn't. My heart split in two and I felt the break. It was visceral and burning.

"I have to go." She said, tenderness creeping through her pained exterior.

"Will I at least see you at graduation? Hal and Joe will want to see you. To say... goodbye."

"No. I'll be too busy unpacking."

"Okay."

"Okay."

"I love you," I said.

"Me too, but it was never meant to be." She put the phone down.

I screamed in the phone booth and punched the glass. It didn't so much as crack and that made me even angrier. I left the phone hanging from its wire and threw myself back in the car. I was so numb that I didn't question my direction until I arrived at school. The ceremony was in an hour or so, but I sat in the car until I saw families start to arrive. I looked down at my crumpled suit and considered driving away, but something deep inside told me that if I could do this, life without May would work out. I needed to take the leap.

We sat with Lynn's family in the crowd. Hal and his parents sat just behind us. We exchanged smiles but nothing more. Joe had graduated the year before but came to watch, sneaking in at the back. Finn's seat was empty. They rattled through all the names and I saw my friends go up and get their diplomas. It seemed almost normal. I got my diploma with modest applause and wiped away a frustrated tear as May's name was called and she didn't appear. They called her again and a murmur went through the crowd. Suddenly I shot up.

"I'll take it!" I said loudly. Everyone stared at me. "I'm her friend. I'll take it to her!" Lynn grabbed my sleeve.

"Sam, sit down!" She said through gritted teeth. I shook her off and ran up onto the stage. The principal looked confused but gave me the scroll. He probably wanted to get on with the unending list of names. Adrenaline coursed through me as I sat back down. My parents seemed embarrassed and Lynn glared at me. "You've got to let her go." She whispered harshly.

Hal graduated top of the class and at the end of the ceremony, he was invited to give the valedictorian speech. As he made his way to the stage, I noticed how smart he looked, considering how little sleep he would have had and the bruising over his nose. I wondered how he'd explained it to his mother. His suit was grey with a tie in the school colours of red and gold. He looked every bit himself. Last night had been terrible but I could see a sense of relief in him now.

When he reached the podium he cleared his throat and stared out anxiously. My best friend was so articulate when it was just us, but large crowds made him anxious. We locked eyes and I nodded at him, smiling gently. He took out his notecards and cleared his throat again, a smile forming over his worried face.

"For those of you who don't know, my name is Henry Burbank..." He spoke about the achievements of the class and quoted President Kennedy and discussed how bright the future was for us all. Towards the end, he looked at me again. "Before I go and leave you to your celebrations, I wanted to finally say thank you to my friends. It hasn't been easy for them to... always be my friend, but they've stuck by me throughout everything... so... thank you." He was given a long round of applause and a standing ovation.

My parents asked me if I wanted to go out for pizza that night but I instead asked them if we could go to Hal's for dinner. When we arrived, the lights were on and I could smell homemade food wafting out the open windows. I knocked on the door and Mrs Burbank greeted us with delight. I walked into the warmly lit dining room and saw that Joe had also been invited. We ate far too much of Mrs Burbank's wonderful cooking and then the three of us excused ourselves and walked down to the den.

The summer heat was melting away from the day and the evening was much cooler. The sun peeked through the trees on the way down the track and we talked and laughed as if nothing had changed. Joe told us that he was moving back to New York to work with his brothers in a mechanic shop. He seemed pretty excited about it and we were glad for him. When it started to get dark, he said goodbye and left, saluting us as he disappeared down the road.

Hal and I sat for a while, talking about who we'd miss from school and where we thought they'd end up. Neither of us mentioned the night before. There was no need; everything had been said. He asked me about May, and I told him she'd decided to move. I never told him what actually happened that night, but I think he had some idea. We said goodbye, though it wasn't sad. We'd see each other again.

I stayed in the den by myself for about an hour. The night was getting colder so I wrapped myself in a blanket. My heart had been made and broken a hundred times in the last 24 hours, but I felt somewhat peaceful.

I didn't see May again for 11 years. I'd taken her diploma to her sister's house but June informed me that May was already gone. She wouldn't tell me where she went.

August, 1973

The house was bigger than I'd expected. Soft blue panelling with white trim and stylish bay windows that I could see were adorned with cream curtains on the inside. It was every bit the suburban dream.

I was nervous as the man opened the door, but once I explained who I was, he smiled brightly and welcomed me into a cosy but spacious kitchen. He was tall and well built, with shockingly white teeth and a neat moustache.
"Have I come at a bad time?" I asked anxiously.
"No, not at all. Delilah's expecting you, she just had to get the kids from my mom's. I'm Darrell by the way!" He spoke with a strong, southern drawl. I nodded and tapped my foot nervously. "Can I get you a drink?" he asked.
"No, thank you. But, do you mind if I use your bathroom? It was a long trip."
"Up the stairs, first door on the left."
I thanked him and made my way upstairs. The stairwell and landing were covered in pictures. Children's drawings interspersed with the odd family photograph.

I didn't go to the bathroom. Instead, I found my way into the master bedroom and sat down on the bed. There were a pair of bedside tables in tasteful but boring cream. The left was obviously Darrell's. A pair of thick-rimmed glasses and a stack of books about succeeding in business adorned the top. The other table held an alarm clock and a marble patterned hairbrush. I was distracted and didn't notice she was there until I heard the door shut.

"Nosey!" The familiar voice startled me and I jumped around. I didn't speak. Just stared at her. Her smirk gleamed back at me through pink lips, and she stood with her hands on her hips. Other than that, she was unrecognisable. I realised that I'd seen her in the family pictures on the stairs, but I hadn't noticed. Age had softened her curves, but her figure was still as perfect as I remembered. She wore loose jeans and a white, summery blouse, and her hair was long and wavy, gathered together at the nape of her neck with a tortoiseshell clip. A different woman altogether.

"May..." My words faltered.

"Delilah."

"Sorry. Delilah." She had told me in her letter that she'd adopted her middle name after leaving the state. She didn't want my brother to find her.

"You came."

"Of course I came. What did you want to talk to me about?"

"It's easier if I show you." She held out her hand and I took it. She led me downstairs and out through some patio doors into a large and neatly kept garden. There was a swing set in the far corner, and three children were running about, chasing a little dog.

"You didn't tell me you had kids M... Delilah."

"There never seemed like a good time." We sat on a small bench on a neatly paved patio.

"How about when I was telling you about mine?" I laughed nervously and she gave an attempt at a smile. "What are their names?" I asked, trying to comprehend her motherhood.

Just then, Darrell appeared from the kitchen. "Honey, I'm off to fill up the car. Don't want to run out of gas halfway to Ohio!" He winked. "Nice meeting ya Sam!" He gave a mock salute and disappeared.

"Darrell is a window salesman. Travels a lot." May explained. She fiddled with her sleeve. We sat in silence for a few minutes until she suddenly exclaimed, "Andrew."

"Sorry?"

"My kids. My youngest, Andrew, is on the swing. He's 5. Michelle is 7, she's trying to catch Pepper." She indicated to a dark-haired little boy, happily kicking his legs on the swing and a similarly dark-haired girl who was racing around the garden after the dog. "And that's Sam." She

pointed to the older boy, who was pushing his brother on the swing. "He'll be 11 soon."
I smiled at the trio. "They're lovely."
We didn't speak for another few minutes.

"Does Lynn know you're here?"
"No..." I rubbed my neck awkwardly, suddenly very warm. "I told her that the company needed me in their Virginia office for the weekend." She said nothing. "I think she was glad of a final bit of peace and quiet before the baby comes. The twins can be a handful but I'm the worst!" I was rambling; trying to fill the decade-long silence between us. "She's due in three months. We're both hoping for a boy. Then I'll be slightly less outnumbered!" I stopped as I noticed the tears falling down May's cheeks. "What? What's wrong?" I reached for her hand but she swiftly pulled it away and wiped her eyes furiously.

"Isn't it crazy? How much everything has changed?" She smiled weakly and stared ahead, the memories playing out in front of her eyes.
"Why are you upset, May?" I didn't correct myself this time. "You've gotta give me some sort of clue here. After getting your letter... I was so happy. But you're not giving anything away. Are you in trouble? Do you need something?"
"A long time ago... maybe we could have had this life." She gestured at her kids. "Once upon a time." She patted my hand and shook her head. "No, I'm not in any trouble."
"Then why am I here?"
"Haven't you worked it out yet?" Suddenly, the little girl was by her side.
"Mommy!" She tugged at May's arm. "The ice cream van! I can hear it! Please, mom, pleaaaaase!" May planted a kiss on Michelle's head and called out to her boys, "Sam! Take your brother and sister to get some ice cream, will ya?" The boy helped his brother off the swing. "Here," she fished a few bucks out of her pocket and gave them to Sam. "Would

ya get me a Choc-Ice and one for my friend here?" He smiled and nodded, his ginger hair flashing in the sunlight. Then with a scurry of spindly legs, they disappeared out of a side gate and onto the street.

May was looking at me, willing me to understand. She sucked in air through her teeth and cleared her throat.
"He's your son, Sam."

I was winded. My breath wouldn't come. I tried to focus on what I could remember of the boy's face.
"He can't be..."
May pulled a photograph from her jeans and handed it to me. The timeline made sense. He was nearly 11. I thought back to that night in the den. But another thought was weighing heavily on my mind and grew even bigger as I looked at the boy's smiling face in the photograph. "May... it wasn't just me who... on that day. I'm sorry..."
"I know. He's the spitting image of him." I started to speak but she interrupted me. "But if you spend any amount of time with him, you'll see. He's got your temperament. Not his. I know he's your son."

Darrell came back around five, and May cooked pasta primavera while we drank beer on the porch. We made small talk. He told me about his job and explained the benefits of double glazing until I glazed over. I asked how they'd met, and he told me how he'd been knocking on doors and handing out leaflets about, you've guessed it, double glazing, and she'd answered the door to her friend's house a few streets away from where they lived now. She'd been over with Sam for a playdate. "I snapped her up straight away." He smiled broadly.
I smiled dryly and finished my beer. "It never bothered you, yanno..."
"The kid? Nah. I fell in love. And Sam's a good kid. Shame about the father." He cracked open another can.
I cleared my throat nervously. "What about him?"

"Delilah said he was no good. Didn't want anything to do with her." He leaned over and patted me on the back, "She also told me you were a good friend to her when y'all were kids. I'm glad she had someone sensible around! Say, you wouldn't happen to know the father would ya? Only, Delilah said he was around when y'all were young." He looked at me expectantly.
I shook my head. "No, we'd... drifted apart by then." I waited for him to question me further, but he leaned back against the porch lazily. We sat in silence, listening to the busy cicadas and the gentle hum of a neighbour's lawnmower.

I thought about the boy. Sam. My son. The words didn't sit right in my head. My family was complete. Lynn and I had been married for seven years. Theresa and Carol were almost 6 and James or Joanna was nearly here. Lynn didn't want any more, although she'd said that after the twins, and I hadn't been bothered either way. But this little boy... where did he fit in? It was still weighing heavily on my mind that there was just as much of a chance of him being my brother's, but May was so certain. Was it the truth, or had she convinced herself of it because the alternative was too painful? The ginger hair, the spray of tiny freckles across his nose... he looked every bit Finn's duplicate. But there was something about his quiet acknowledgement of me earlier that struck differently. I couldn't find any answers on this porch.

May called us in for food, but I wasn't hungry. I made a hasty excuse about having to check into the hotel and left without saying a proper goodbye. She let me go. Darrell protested a little, in his old-fashioned southern way, saying it would be no bother for me to stay in their guest room, but I said I'd already paid. I waved a wooden hand at the kids and walked out to my car. I sat in the driver's seat for a few moments, staring blankly at the keys in my hand, trying to remember their purpose.

A light tap on the window startled me. I gestured to the passenger seat and May got in.
"Don't go." She said.
"I have to. I'm sorry. I can't do this."
"I'm not asking you to *do* anything Sam. Just stay for some pasta. What's the harm?"
"There's more harm here than you seem to realise." I turned the keys in the ignition. "I have to go."
"You don't."
The whole afternoon suddenly hit me square in the face. "Get out of the car May. You can't just do things like this to people."
"Sam..." She put her arms around me, but I shrugged her off.
"Get out." I was angry. Angry at her for springing this on me. Angry that she hid it in the first place. Angry that this kid was growing up in a web of lies. She didn't move. "Get out of the FUCKING CAR!" I yelled, slamming my hands into the wheel. She jumped but remained calm.
"Just come in and talk to him properly."
I turned to face her. "What's your angle here May? Gonna tell him his dad suddenly wants to know him, huh? What are you planning on telling your husband?"
"I... just wanted to get you here. I didn't think past that."
"Of course you didn't. You never think of anyone but yourself." I put the car into gear. "Get. Out."
I left her there on the porch in front of her house. As I drove away, I saw Darrell come out. May hastily wiped away a tear and took his hand, leading him back inside.

I didn't go to the hotel. Instead, I drove around the suburban streets, past immaculately manicured front gardens leading to large houses in pastel colours. My whole life was playing out in front of my eyes. Every moment with the gang. Each knee scrape and summer sleepover. Joe and May. Kevin's grave. Waving goodbye to Don. Lynn. Hal. Finn. That night.

I pulled off the main road into a quiet side street and heaved against my back wheel, though nothing came up. I sat heavily against a tree stump and cried. When I finally checked my watch it was 21:36, so I decided to go to the hotel.

After checking in I went to the hotel bar and chased down a whiskey with another and a bag of peanut M&Ms that cost almost as much as the room had. I didn't drink much, other than socially, but the mess of my mind needed numbing. The M&Ms were just... because. About an hour later I found myself plodding down the paisley carpeted corridor to my room. I flopped on the bed, and the next thing I knew, a shrill ringing filled the chincy honeymoon deluxe suite- the only room available at such short notice. I held the receiver to my ear.

"Sorry, to disturb you at this hour, sir," The nasally voice of the nighttime receptionist was loud and uncomfortable compared to the silence of the room. I looked at my watch; it had just gone midnight. "There's a caller on the line, and they say it's urgent." My first thought was May. Had Darrell figured it all out and turned on her? Guilt flooded in. Why hadn't my mind gone straight to my pregnant wife? Or my daughters? "Sir..?"

"Yes, sorry, put them through," I said groggily, rubbing my forehead with my thumb and index finger.

"Right away sir." The line clicked a few times, and then the crackly sound of far-away breathing filled my ears.

"Hello?" I waited.

"Sam." May. I gripped the phone tightly, my knuckles turning white.

"Is everything okay?" I cleared my throat, the taste of alcohol still present and biting on my tongue. She didn't say anything. "I'm sorry... how I acted earlier... I was confused."

Her voice smiled wryly. "I know. I shoulda given you more time." A thought struck me.

"Why now, May? This kid has been around for 10 years. Why did you send me a letter last month, and not when he was born?"
Silence.
I could hear her breathing shakily. "I didn't think there was time."
"What? Time for what?"
"Can you come back?" Her voice was a whisper.
"I'm drunk."
"I'll call you a cab."
"Okay." There was nothing to say. She had angered me and was confusing me now, but I didn't want to stay in this room. I wanted to see her. To hear her explanations. She still pulled me in. I felt the urge to fix everything for her. I was 12, 15, 18 and in love.

I was standing outside her house again by 1:30. She quietly let me in and we went back outside to the bench we had been sat on earlier.
"I need you to give it to me straight, May. You wrote me a letter. Asked me here. I've done what you've asked. Please. Just tell me the whole truth."
She looked at me in that way she always did, a smile in her eyes, but it didn't reach her mouth this time. She took a deep breath. "I'll say it all. Promise me you won't interrupt until I'm done."
I nodded. "Okay."
"When I left, after staying with my sister, I didn't know. It was only a few months after. Two... three maybe? I wasn't sick. Just felt a bit... strange. I didn't tell June who the father was, just said it was some local guy. At that point... I didn't know. It was an equal chance. But yanno, I prayed every day that it was you. I never doubted I'd love the kid, either way. Just didn't want to see... him, every time I looked at my baby." She put her hands up in surrender. "I know what you're thinking. I do see your brother in him. But it's easy to see past that when he is every bit your son. He's so quiet. And sweet. And smart too. I just know, Sam."

She adjusted her legs and sat with them crossed in front, facing me on the bench. "I thought about telling you when he was born, but when he was small I still wasn't sure he was yours. It wasn't until he was a toddler that the You in him shone through. And by then you were married... It didn't seem right." She stopped as if she'd finished.
"That doesn't answer my question."
"No, I guess not. The truth is, I probably wouldn't have told you. Ever. But then... I had to. There wasn't enough time." She'd said that over the phone.
"Enough time for what?" I probed gently.
"For me."

She never knew, but those two words ripped straight through me. It was a pain I'd never felt before. Pure fear boiled my blood, and I had to fight to keep from vomiting. But she sat there and explained to me that her radiotherapy had worked. The cancer was gone. She explained how scared they'd all been when the tumour got bigger, and how she'd decided to tell me about Sam before it was... too late. She'd sent the letter after her final treatment, then found out two weeks later that the tumour was gone.
"The damage was done." She said. "I knew it was the right thing to do. You deserved to know." She burst into tears and I pulled her into my arms like I had all those years ago. Her bright eyes looked up at mine and I saw what she had seen earlier- the fleeting chance of our life together. It was something I chose to hide away inside the darkest corners of my mind. I'd ignored the longing for as long as I could, but her letter had stirred up those painful and beautiful feelings and thrown me into such turmoil that I had to pick at the old wound. And now, with the news about my son and May's illness, I knew that my two worlds would have to collide and coexist. I had no idea how Lynn would react. I was sure that she'd feel betrayed. No matter my motives, I had been unfaithful, and now there was living breathing evidence of my infidelity that couldn't be ignored. The idea

of a big family meal including May and my son seemed ridiculous. I had no idea how I would ever make it work.

"I'm so sorry Sam." She said.
"Don't be. It's a shock, sure, but I'm just so relieved that you're okay. And if what you've told me about little Sam is true then I know I'll grow to love him as you do."
She brightened at this. "You want to know him?" I nodded and she leaned forward and kissed me softly. For a moment, I let it happen. This was what I had always wanted. But then, the memories of before flashed in front of my eyes again. I saw the seven of us, that summer before Kevin's death. We were enthralled in one of May's stories and from my outside perspective, I saw how each of us loved her with everything we had. The twins were so young that they looked up to her like an older sister. They didn't have anyone else in town who made them feel safe and loved. Joe yearned for her fieriness and her body. For those few months they were together, they existed within their own bubble of desire because they balanced each other out with fierce passion and tender joy. Hal felt understood by her. She saw past his shame and allowed him to be completely himself without fear. Finn loved her as Joe did, but without the connection of two identical souls. He simply wanted her as a prize, and his love turned violent in the end. I could see my small figure, leaning toward May as she spoke. I loved her with my whole being and her light encompassed me and made the very mediocre trajectory of my life seem worth living.

But that was then.

We had all suffered so much loss since that day. Back in May's garden as she kissed me in the moonlight, I realised that my love for her was no longer so strong that it hurt. I would always love her. First love never dies. But the all-consuming power she'd always had over me was gone. I was a married man- married to a woman I loved as deeply

as I could- and the overwhelming love I'd felt for her had transferred to my children the second my twins had first stretched out their starfish hands towards me.
I felt calm. The same calm I'd experienced that last night at the den. I'd known then that my life without May was not only possible but would be full of happiness. The same assured feeling crept over me now, and I pulled away from the kiss.
"We're not going to do this," I said, taking her hand.
"No... you're right." She smiled at me sadly. "We don't need each other anymore. All this time, I've been holding on to the idea of us because we never got to say goodbye. We didn't fight or have a final fuck, or even just drift. But I..."
"You had to go."
"Yes."
"And now, so do I." So I did.

I called a cab and went back to the hotel to collect my things, then drove through the dawn to get home. I kissed my sleeping girls and woke Lynn gently. We sat in the early morning sun out on the porch and I told her everything. She didn't shout or curse or consign me to hell. She just sat and listened until I was through, then stood, her hand resting on her pregnant belly. She turned to me and said, "I was never so naive to think that there was nothing between you and her. I also can't say it won't take me a little while to forgive you... but in the end... after loving her the most, you chose me. And our life hasn't been half bad." I'd taken her in my arms and we'd swayed back and forth to the sounds of crickets chirping.

December 1976

My family and May's family started meeting every month for a BBQ or movie night or something to that effect. Since that fateful summer in 1973 when I'd gained a son, I'd spent a lot of time with him. May had been right. Little Sam was the spit of my brother, but watching the way he moved through life and interacted with people, I knew he was mine. We went fishing occasionally, and sometimes I took all the kids, mine and Sam's half-siblings included, and we'd drive to a lake.

There was no animosity between Lynn and May. They both understood how the past had led them to their current point of happiness and they got along as they did in our days in Iowa. I often wondered if Darrell ever worked out the true relationship between his stepson and me then, but he never mentioned it. It made me feel slightly deceitful, but May had obviously chosen not to tell Darrell for a reason. We also decided we wouldn't reveal anything to Sam until he was older. He was just a kid and didn't need his world rocked just yet.

In December 1976, my family drove to May and Darrell's for Christmas. We ate and drank until almost bursting and the kids played with each other's new toys for hours. Towards bedtime, May gathered the children and read them a story. Young James sandwiched himself between Theresa and Carol, and Andrew and Michelle happily squished in on either side. Sam hung back, fingering the back of the sofa. I put a hand on his shoulder and he walked with me into the hallway.

"What's up kid?" I asked. He had shot up in the last three years and had started on the road to manhood.

"Nothing much... it's just... I overheard mom talking on the telephone the other day. She was saying all this stuff and then I heard my name. And she said something about my father."

"Ah." I didn't quite know what to say.

"I didn't mean to eavesdrop! But mom sounded angry." He said hurriedly. "But I couldn't help it. I heard her pick up a pad of paper and write something down. After she left for work I went in and found the paper. It said, 'Sam and family for Christmas'." He looked at me earnestly. "What I'm asking is... do you know my father?"

My heart started pounding. I knew the exact conversation he had overheard. May and I had been arranging Christmas plans and I'd asked if she thought we should tell Sam about me soon. We'd argued a bit as she'd wanted to wait a few more years.

"All I know," I said, "is that your father didn't know that you'd been born at the time. And I know that if he knew you now, he'd love you very much." He didn't seem satisfied by this, but I'd promised May that I'd wait until his 15th birthday. "Come on," I said. "I think Auntie Lynn might be opening the chocolates."

When we went back in, May looked up at us and I shook my head softly to indicate our secret was still safe. She smiled and stood, but I noticed her wincing as she did so.

1977

In January, May looked very tired when we all came down to visit. She didn't engage much in the conversation but blamed it on the flu.

In February and March, she seemed much the same, but in April our weekend was cancelled because she was sick.

In May, she fainted whilst at work and was rushed to hospital where tests were done that discovered her tumour was back and much bigger than before.

Thanks to the chemotherapy, June and July were earmarked for numerous trips to visit her in hospital. Her hair fell out and she was so thin I could see her bones.

She remained positive throughout August, which kept us all going, but September and October went by with no improvement and by November, she was given less than a year to live.

I took this in as Darrell sobbed the news down the phone. Lynn and I agreed to drive down to help him with the kids that weekend while he sorted everything out. May had been allowed back home and she tried to pretend everything was normal. I don't think the younger kids understood too much, but Sam did. He was constantly hovering over his mother in case she fell or was out of breath.

We continued to visit every month, as they couldn't easily come to us anymore, and I watched as she grew weaker and weaker. She would get angry when she thought no one was around and she would sit up all night sometimes watching the children sleep top and toe, all piled in together.

1978

I'll pause here, because May dies in 1978. I'll tell you all about that soon, but this story isn't just hers and mine.

After my graduation, Hal, Joe and Finn went out into the world too. The reason I'm interjecting them now is that we reconvened in 1978 for May's funeral and I got to see them again properly.

Starting with my brother, I didn't speak to him for the month that elapsed between my graduation and my moving away to join our uncle's company. His football days were well behind him and there was nothing on the horizon for him so he'd started working in the local butcher's shop, and that's where he remained until he died. No wife or kids. No house. He stayed with my parents and bled them dry. When I'd visited home over the years, he'd always been out or passed out in his bedroom, high. The coke had ruined his nose and his brain and all that remained was the anger and resentment he felt towards me.

Joe had done much better. He'd gone back to New York like he'd said and eventually became manager of the mechanics where he worked. He met a nice girl named Rosa and they had four sons. We wrote to each other every so often, but visiting never seemed appropriate. He was doing better than Finn, but he took no shit and that made him unpopular with clients. They were poor and it felt unkind to impose on him. I guess I also still felt inferior to him. When he'd sent me a picture of him and his family, he'd looked exactly the same, just broader.

And then there was Hal. He'd gotten into all of his first-choice colleges but decided on Yale. He and I left town on the same day, him to Connecticut and me to Chicago. We saw each other a few times, but I let the friendship fade. There was still a part of me that was deeply uncomfortable with who he was and I wanted simplicity. He seemed happy enough to allow our communication to fall by the wayside too. I think that I was a reminder of the vulnerability he'd felt in Iowa and my actions on prom night had scarred him forever. Both of us wanted to keep the memories of life before that night, so my best friend and I moved on.

Whether it was through hatred, fear or love, I lost my remaining friends to the world for a time. On the day of May's funeral, however, I saw them sitting far apart in the crowd as I stood to give the eulogy. Finn sat at the very back of the church, his head bent low, not catching my eye. Joe was seated in the middle row, his suit faded but pressed neatly. Hal looked up at me from close to the front. He was behind Darrell and the kids. May had asked me to invite them all. Despite my misgivings, I'd sent each of them the details of the funeral. I'd deliberated for days about inviting my brother because of all the pain he'd caused, but May had taken me by the hand and said, "I want him to see the joy I've had despite what he took."

At the podium, I cleared my throat. I found myself looking to Hal for reassurance, as he had at the graduation. Darrell had asked me to give the eulogy, as he knew he'd never be able to get through it, and I'd agreed.

"As some of you will know, May and I were friends for years." I began. "She marched into my life at 14 and it hasn't been the same since. The seven of us... our friends... we used to visit a den we built almost every day. May brought us laughter and happiness and looked out for us all the time. We all cared for her deeply. But when she moved away, we all seemed to lose touch. Then fate, or God, or whatever you want to call it brought my friend back to me, and for that, I will be forever grateful, because not only did I get to feel May's warmth again, but I had the pleasure of meeting her husband and children too. She was a joy to everyone who knew and loved her, and she was full of surprises..." I took a piece of paper out of my jacket pocket. "Before she passed, May gave me this note that she wanted me to read today. She made me promise not to look at it until now, so here we go." I unfolded the paper and smoothed it out, my fingers running across familiar but shaky handwriting.

My mind flashed back to the moment a few months earlier when May had given me the paper. Towards the end of June, she knew her time was running out so she'd asked me if I would take her back to Iowa to revisit the past one last time. I'd been hesitant, not wanting to bring up any painful memories- for either of us- but she'd insisted, saying "How can you say no to a dying woman?" with that familiar twinkle in her eyes.

We'd gone with both families, but May took the kids and Darrell to stay with her sister June in the city and Lynn, the twins, James and I stayed with Lynn's parents. We visited the school and drove past Kevin and Don's old house and spent hours walking through Des Moines, commenting on all the changes. May had a special request for the last night, so after Lynn and I had dinner with my mom and dad- making sure Finn was out- I drove back to the city to pick her up. We drove back and parked by the track that led to where the den had once been. I didn't expect it to be there anymore.

May had insisted we do this alone, but it was hard getting her down the track as she was so weak. She leaned heavily on my arm and we had to stop multiple times. After struggling down the bank, we both stopped and stared. It was still there. The curtain had been removed from the doorway and the tarp from the roof was gone, but the skeleton of the den was intact. Inside, the stools were there along with some food wrappers, showing that other kids had found our hideout.

"I'm glad it's being used," I said.

May smiled at me. "I don't think they're down here as much as we were." She was right, the carpet was very damp and almost completely black and the wood at the other end had rotted so much that it had created a back entrance. "Do you know what's funny?" She said. I shook my head, puzzled. "I never even considered asking if you had protection that night."

I laughed loudly. "That's very true. I didn't have any anyway." We both laughed again.

"I guess little Sam was meant to be." She looked off out of the hole in the wall, wistfully.

I was suddenly overcome by an immense sadness. "I don't want you to leave us."

"Oh, sweetie... I don't want to go." We hugged each other tightly, and I cried into her thin shoulder. She pulled away and looked at me intently. "I need you to do something for me."

"Anything."

"When it's time for you to... wave me off, read this. I want you all to know how deeply I love you. All of you. Okay? Promise you won't read it until the funeral? I don't like goodbyes. I need you to do this." I promised and tucked the paper into my pocket. "There's something for the others in there... if they come."

They had come. I was looking out at them now. Finn, Joe and Hal. I looked down at the paper again, taking a second to skim the words.

"This is what May wrote. Darrell, my love, thank you for bringing me hope and stability all these years. You are a good man. I love you and I will miss you. Take care of my babies." Darrell beamed at me through his tears, grasping his children close. "Andrew, keep working hard on your drawings and look after your sister. Michelle, promise you'll stay in school and work really hard. Little Sam, you're not alone." The children were silent and sad. "Lynn and my lovely nieces and nephew, thank you for bringing big Sam back into my life along with your love." The list went on like this, naming people I didn't know, explaining how much they meant to her. Then, towards the bottom I reached us. I felt a lump rise in my throat. "Finn, what we had was wrong, but look at what I ended up with despite it all. Remember that." I stared at my brother. He didn't look up or acknowledge the words once. "Joe, what we had was fun and I'm glad you were my first. I hope you are too." Joe shuffled uneasily but nodded at me, letting me know he had taken it in. "Hal, my dear sweet friend... look after yourself. Trust that the world won't always look like this." Hal's face was marked by tears, but he didn't wipe them away. Tears pricked behind my eyes too as I read the final line. "Sam... every time I've told you how I've felt, I've meant it. Don't be nervous about reading this, Darrell knows." I glanced at him and he smiled reassuringly. "We were never meant to be but I'm so glad that we were... something, all this time. You'll go on without me just fine. Thanks for this sweetie."

Finn slunk away straight after the service, but Joe and Hal stayed for a while. We talked over sausage rolls and relayed as much of the last 16 years that letters hadn't covered. It was somewhat stiff, as it always is with old friends, but I was glad to see them again. At the wake, Sam wouldn't catch my eye. He kept looking between Darrell and me. When people started to leave I took him to one side and asked if he was alright. I cut him a generous slice of cake from the buffet and we went outside and sat on a bench that had been erected to remember someone else. "So, you and my mom were..." He asked.

"Yeah..."

"Were you still together when she met Darrell?"

"No, no. We'd lost touch years before that, don't you worry." I sounded awkward like I was trying too hard.

“Okay.” I could sense he wanted to ask me the big question. He didn’t look at me, just stared out at the sunset. It felt as if the evening was holding its breath. “Are you my father?”

I let out a sigh five years in the making. “Yes.”

Sam nodded, still looking at the fading sun. His face crumpled and I put a kind hand on his shoulder, turning my face away to hide my own tears. I think he understood, even then, that nothing had been hidden from him out of spite. Any son of May could never believe she would hurt him deliberately. We’ve spoken about it all many times since that day, and I think he’s made his peace with it. He is now married with two beautiful daughters of his own, May and Delilah.

We see each other often. We continued the monthly visits, and in the end, Darrell moved with the kids to Illinois so we’d be close. I took everyone to Iowa again a few weeks after the funeral to sprinkle her ashes where she wanted to finally be at rest- in the river that flowed past our den.

Once the children had grown and fled the nest, Darrell found love again. A kind woman named Queenie who baked the most amazing pies for thanksgiving. They’ve both passed on now.

So has my brother, though that didn’t hit me as hard. Darrell was more of a brother to me than Finn ever was. He had a heart attack at 51, thanks to years of cocaine and guilt pressing on his heart. His death meant that the house in Iowa where we had grown up passed to me. It had been willed to Finn by my parents years ago and then to me if he never bothered to do anything with it. Lynn and I considered moving back, but the small town seemed too far in the past. Outside of my memories, it didn’t exist at all in our lives. So we visited to pack up the rooms and sold it. Finn is buried in the town cemetery. Just over the fence from his grave lies Kevin.

Joe died in his sleep just last year. We'd gone fishing that summer of 1978. After the funeral, we'd kept in touch more and I'd finally gone to see him in New York. The poverty I'd imagined was far from the truth and his life seemed to have worked out exactly as he needed it to. I miss his no fucks attitude and the large presence he filled every space with.

And, of course, my best friend. Hal. I saw him slightly more than Joe, as he flew to Chicago often for work. He was an investment banker, stationed in Nevada. He never married or put up any pretence of that sort, so we never spoke of love. Even when my son James came out to us all over dinner one night and I finally opened my heart and mind to his partner, Hal and I never spoke of it. He'd always understood me better than I understood myself and he saw the change without me having to show it. Hal doesn't have a happy ending. He has a happy start and an okay middle but the end... that came too soon.

In 1985 I received a call from Joe, explaining that Hal had been due to visit him but never showed up. He'd made some calls and discovered that Hal had been arrested in Nevada for public indecency. The charges had been further brought up to include two counts of sodomy. I wrote to Hal in prison, but never got a reply. Two months later, a formal letter from Nevada State Prison arrived, which informed me that Henry Burbank had committed suicide by hanging in his cell at the age of 39. I was listed as his forwarding address and would be responsible for the collection of his belongings and body.

As I never found out what happened to Don, I'm the last of the seven of us left. You might think that it makes me feel lonely. Sometimes I think about my friends and my years in the den and I get sad. But I'm not lonely. I have my wife and my children and grandchildren, and despite the pain that my story holds, May was right. I went on without her just fine.

www.ingramcontent.com/pod-product-compliance
Lightning Source LLC
LaVergne TN
LVHW090131160826
845673LV00017B/2064

* 9 7 9 8 8 4 1 2 2 3 1 4 6 *